RESTLESS WOLF

WOLVES OF BLACKPINE™
BOOK TWO

RIVER TATUM

MICHAEL ANDERLE

FLORID Romance

DON'T MISS OUR NEW RELEASES

Join the Florid Romance email list to be notified of new releases and special promotions (which happen often) by following this link:

https://floridromance.lmbpn.com/about/sign-up-for-our-newsletter/

Published by Florid Romance
an imprint of LMBPN Publishing
2375 E. Tropicana Avenue, Suite 8-305
Las Vegas, Nevada 89119 USA

Version 1.00, April 2026
eBook ISBN: 979-8-89790-229-3
Print ISBN: 979-8-89790-230-9

ONE

COMING HOME

The bell above the door had needed oiling since approximately the second Clinton administration.

Lily Thornton was aware of this fact, as she had communicated it to her grandfather at the ages of nine, fourteen, and once more at twenty-two, at which time she considered it her final gesture of assistance before her permanent return to Bozeman. Earl had said *mm* on each occasion in the tone that meant, *I have heard you, and I won't be doing anything about it.* The bell still wasn't oiled. It announced her arrival now with the same arthritic shriek it had produced her entire childhood. Earl looked up from behind the counter with an expression that hadn't meaningfully changed in thirty years.

"Bell needs oiling," Lily said.

"Mm," Earl responded.

She set her bag down on the wooden floor, scuffed and familiar, the grain worn pale in the paths people walked most, and looked around. Wooden floors. Tin ceiling.

Shelves crowded with everything from motor oil to paperback novels, a cast-iron stove radiating heat from the far corner. The store smelled the way it had always smelled, a combination of wood and dust and stock that she had been carrying in some archive of her body for eight years without knowing it, because walking through the door released it all at once.

Nothing had changed. This was either comforting or unbearable, and she hadn't yet decided which.

"Dottie's upstairs," Earl said. "Told her you were coming. She said she knew."

"Of course she did."

She had driven from Bozeman that morning, four hours on roads that went from interstate to highway to the two-lane that wound up through the mountains. The last twenty miles were the familiar ones. The switchback that looked like it would drop you off the edge and didn't, the pine break where the valley opened up, the water tower at the edge of town that still leaned three degrees to the left. She had left at eighteen and come back for holidays and left again and come back for one more holiday and left again, and each time the water tower leaned exactly the same way, indifferent to the years.

The town was small like mountain towns, not cramped but concentrated, buildings pulled close against the cold. Blackpine had roughly twenty-four hundred people and the settled character of a place that had been here long enough not to need to explain itself. The mountains had been here longer. The pines had been here longer. The Thornton General Store had been here since before the county had a formal record of it, according to Earl, who wasn't given to embellishment.

Lily went upstairs.

DOTTIE WAS in the armchair by the window with a book open on her lap and the expression of a woman who had been expecting this for some time.

"You look tired," she said.

"I drove four hours."

"You looked tired before that." Dottie's eyes were sharp under her steel-gray hair, the same eyes she'd always had, eyes that saw the truth behind the surface. "Sit down. Stop hovering in the doorway like you're waiting to be dismissed."

Lily sat. Dottie looked her over with frank, unsoftened assessment, seventy-odd years of it, and she had stopped cushioning the results. Then she reached a conclusion she found acceptable.

"The doctor says I'm ahead of schedule," Dottie said.

"I know. He called me."

"Then you know I didn't need you to drive four hours."

"I know you didn't need me to." Lily looked at her grandmother, the cardigan, the book, how she held herself in the chair, careful and deliberate, taking it easy on her own terms. The physician used terms such as *"mild stroke"* and *"good recovery trajectory,"* which provided reassurance, though she recognized these expressions from prior emergency room visits, where their accuracy later proved insufficient. "I wanted to come."

"Mm," Dottie said, which in Dottie's vocabulary meant, *I know. I'm glad. I'm not going to make a thing of it.*

Lily had grown up parsing the *mm* that was her grand-father's entire vocabulary. She had also grown up parsing its variant in Dottie, which was warmer and contained a different category of information.

"You'll be sleeping in your old room," Dottie said. "The bedding's clean. Your grandfather did it this morning, which means it's slightly rumpled because he doesn't make beds as anyone else makes beds, but the sheets are fresh."

"That's fine."

"Ask me what I want to know," Dottie said in the same way she said everything, not a question but a statement delivered at the appropriate moment.

Lily looked up. "What do you want to know?"

"If you're all right." She put the question down between them. "Not about the drive. Not about the job. If you're all right."

Lily considered. She had spent six years in emergency medicine in Bozeman, which was a city with a hospital that had a genuine trauma unit and a patient load that justified it. She had been good at the work. She had been, she thought, genuinely satisfied by the work as you were satisfied by work that used the full capacity of what you were. About eight months ago, the satisfaction stopped. She left a twelve-hour shift, went home, and after two hours called Earl to see if he needed help at the store.

Earl had said *"mm"* in a tone that meant, *"I was wondering when you'd ask."*

She had taken a leave of absence. She had told herself it was temporary.

"I'm fine," she said.

Dottie looked at her. "Ask me about the Mercers," she said instead.

Lily paused. This wasn't the question she had expected. "What about the Mercers?"

"You're thinking about them. You always did, when you came back. How you'd watch for the Mercer boys from the store window when you thought no one was watching." The faintest trace that might have been amusement crossed Dottie's face. "So ask me."

"What would you tell me?"

"Not much." A flat statement, the answer complete as given. "Not yet. But when you've been here a while, when you've settled in and paid attention, you'll see." She turned back to her book in a way that meant the conversation was over, which was another skill Dottie excelled at, the conclusive pivot. "There are worse fates than a place that knows how to keep its own."

Lily went back downstairs.

She was on the step stool at quarter past twelve, reaching for a misplaced can of tomato paste on the upper shelf, when the bell rang.

She had learned the step stool's wobble in the first

hour (left leg; weight needed to be centered), and she finished placing the can before coming down. She turned.

The man inside the door had stopped.

This wasn't a routine pause; rather, it was an intentional halt by a man prepared for the situation. He was broad across the shoulders and wearing a jacket with the BWR logo, Blackpine Wilderness Rescue, the same one she had seen on Cole Mercer a hundred times over the years. He had sandy-brown hair that looked like his hand had run through it recently and hadn't quite recovered. He needed a shave. He was tall, like people who didn't think about it.

She knew him.

The recognition took a moment, faces changed in eight years and settled into different shapes, but she had grown up seeing Jace Mercer at the edges of every summer, the younger Mercer brother, the one who made things easy. The one who remembered names and smoothed things over with a smile that made people feel the room was better for having him in it. He had been part of the furniture of her Blackpine summers as the mountains were, constant and present.

He had changed. Broader. Quieter, in how he held himself, that hadn't been there when they were teenagers.

He was looking at her.

It wasn't the usual glance of someone sizing up a customer.

"Hi," she said. "Can I help you find anything?"

He blinked. His expression folded back into the warmth she remembered from his face when they were young. "I need—yeah. Batteries." His voice was lower than she remembered, rougher at the edges.

"Aisle three," she said. "Far end, left side."

He nodded, precise, and moved toward aisle three.

She watched him for one second longer than was professionally required before turning back to the inventory sheet.

HE WAS BACK in two minutes.

He set two boxes on the counter. Both C-cells. She looked at them without expression. She couldn't identify a single device in the store, or in any household she could currently account for in Blackpine, that required C-cell batteries with any urgency. He had found the first box his hand touched and committed to it. She was as certain of this as she was of diagnoses before she had the language for them, in her body first, her mind arriving after.

"Six forty-two," she said.

He put a twenty on the counter, picked up the batteries and turned away.

She opened the register. "Do you want change?"

"Keep it." He was already turning toward the door, not quite meeting her eyes. "For the—put it toward the store." He moved through the door with the deliberate nature of someone maintaining a pace they had chosen in advance.

The bell shrieked.

Lily stood at the register with thirteen dollars and

fifty-eight cents in her hand and looked at the space where he had been.

Earl materialized from somewhere in the back with the unhurried timing of a man who had been listening to all of this.

"Jace Mercer," he said. Not a question.

"I know." She had recognized him. It had taken a moment, but she had. "He's changed."

"Time does that." Earl came behind the counter and began going through the afternoon delivery slips without hurrying. "Works with his brother. Has for a while."

"He bought the wrong batteries."

"Mm."

"And he overpaid by thirteen dollars and fifty-eight cents."

"Mm," Earl said, in the tone that meant, *I have a complete opinion about this situation, and I am exercising restraint.*

Lily looked at the money in her hand. "We were close," she said. "When we were kids."

"You were." Earl looked up briefly. "He remembered you. When you'd come back for holidays, before you stopped coming back much." He noted it the way he noted inventory. Fact. Filed. "Good man. Has some matters he's working out."

She waited for more. Earl went back to the delivery slips.

This was what she had always experienced growing up in Blackpine and had never figured out. The town kept its secrets, sharing only what it chose, and waited for you to ask the right questions in the right sequence. Her grandparents did it. Marge at the diner did it. The Mercers did it more than anyone. She had left at eighteen before anyone had handed her the key.

She was back now.

She put the thirteen fifty-eight in the register and went back to the inventory sheet.

THE AFTERNOON BROUGHT three more customers, a delivery from a supplier Earl communicated with exclusively through handwritten notes, and a conversation with a woman named Mrs. Patterson, who had opinions about Lily's altitude adjustment and a printout to support them. Lily listened. She had learned in the ER that listening was almost always more efficient than redirecting, and Mrs. Patterson, once she had delivered her information, turned out to also have twenty years of Blackpine social history stored at conversational pressure and no reluctance to share it.

By three o'clock, Lily knew which families had been in Blackpine the longest, which ones had left and come back, and which ones were what Mrs. Patterson called *original stock,* which meant more than just long tenure. The Mercers were original stock. So were the Thorntons. So were three or four other families whose names Lily tucked away.

"Your grandmother and the Mercer boys' mother were close," Mrs. Patterson said, with the particular emphasis people used when they meant *closer than you'd expect.* "Before she passed." She shook her head. "Cole was twenty-two. Took on a lot."

"I didn't know her well," Lily said. "The mother."

"No, you'd have been young when she got sick." Mrs. Patterson collected her purchases briskly and moved on. "But your grandmother did. Some truths go deeper than what people explain out loud in this town. You'll learn the shape of it." She said it as though it were a fact about geography. "We all do, eventually."

Lily stood at the counter.

She had been hearing versions of that her entire life in Blackpine. As a child, she had accepted it as normal because children accepted the texture of their world. As a nurse, she realized she lacked complete information.

She went back to the delivery manifest and wrote down what she had.

SHE WAS STILL THINKING about it at eleven that night.

Not the batteries, which she had categorized and explained. Not the overpayment. Not Earl's careful non-answer.

The look on his face when he walked through the door.

She grew up knowing the Mercer family was different in ways that Blackpine didn't explain directly. Her grandmother had always been part of the town's inner circle, the people who exchanged looks when certain things were said, who knew which questions to answer and which ones to defer. Her grandfather had run this store for fifty years alongside relationships that went deeper than commerce. She had grown up in the atmosphere of that knowledge without being handed its substance.

She was a nurse. She had spent years in emergency rooms with cases that didn't fit the textbook, and she had learned that the first step wasn't to explain but to observe. To collect data without forcing a framework onto it before the framework was ready.

She had data.

Jace Mercer had walked through that door today knowing she would be there. She was certain of this with the same bodily certainty she brought to diagnoses, not because she could prove it but because the look on his face wasn't the look of surprise. She didn't know what that meant yet.

She was going to find out.

Some choices, Dottie had said, *you never stop wondering about.* She delivered that comment in Dottie's usual style, with statements that reached far beyond the situation at hand.

Lily turned off the light in her childhood bedroom and looked at the ceiling she had looked at for the first eighteen years of her life.

She was supposed to be here for a few months. She was supposed to go back to Bozeman.

She wasn't thinking about Bozeman.

TWO

THE BOLT

He drove past the store four times that week.

Monday, he had told himself he was going to the hardware store. Tuesday was the same. On Wednesday, he had actually gone to the hardware store, bought a box of wood screws he didn't need, and driven past the general store on his way back without slowing. Thursday, he had parked two streets over and talked himself out of it in the span of approximately four minutes before driving home with nothing accomplished.

Friday morning, he parked in front of Thornton General Store and turned off the engine.

His wolf said nothing. It had been silent since Monday, a creature exercising patience it didn't feel, waiting for Jace to reach the conclusion it had already reached. The silence was worse than commentary.

He sat with his hands on the steering wheel and thought about batteries. He was out of batteries. This wasn't true. He had an entire drawer of them, various sizes, because he lived alone in a cabin he had built himself and was precise about household maintenance; he did not run out of batteries. But needing batteries was a reason to go into a general store and have a normal interaction with the person running it, and he was the Beta of the Blackpine Pack, and he had known Earl Thornton for thirty years, and he had legitimate reasons to walk through that door.

He was going to walk through the door and say hello to Lily Thornton, and it was going to be a normal interaction, and he was going to prove to himself that he could do this.

He got out of the truck.

JACE HAD BEEN at HQ reviewing trail reports when Cole came in from the morning run and said, with the economy of someone delivering information they knew would land hard, "Dottie Thornton had a stroke. Lily's coming home."

Jace had looked at the trail map for three seconds. "I know," he said.

Cole had looked at him and then gone back to the reports without further comment. Sometimes *I know* contained everything that needed to be said.

He had known Lily was coming before Cole told him. His wolf had known the moment the decision was made, as it knew facts about the mate bond with a certainty that wasn't the same as human knowing and couldn't be argued with. She hadn't been within range yet. She would be. His wolf had settled into a waiting posture, patient as only absolute certainty could be.

He had known the Thorntons his whole life. Earl had been part of Blackpine's inner circle since before Jace was born, one of the families that had always understood what the Mercers were and kept that knowledge the way Blackpine kept all its essential knowledge, carefully, without making it a burden. He had grown up running trails behind the general store. He had known Lily as the granddaughter who came for summers, the one who noticed things and asked careful questions and listened as some people listened, with their whole attention.

He had told her to go, told her the position was too good to defer, told her he would wait. She had gone. The calls had shortened and stopped, and he had built his wall and made his peace with what wasn't going to happen.

His wolf had known she was his mate, eight months before she came through that door.

He hadn't gone to the store.

THE BELL above the door needed oiling.

Jace had heard it his whole life and had mentioned it to Earl twice in the last three years. Earl had said mm on both occasions. The bell announced him now with the same shriek it had always produced, and he stepped inside.

The store was the same it had always been. Wooden floors worn pale in the walked paths, tin ceiling, shelves dense with stock, the cast-iron stove throwing heat from the corner. It smelled of wood and dust and the layered scent of stock that had been in the same building for generations.

Earl wasn't behind the counter.

Someone was on the step stool at the far end of the aisle, back turned, reaching for the upper shelf. She had strawberry-blonde hair and the stillness of someone focused on the task in front of her.

He knew the set of her shoulders.

He hadn't seen Lily Thornton in eight years, but his wolf had been tracking her by scent since she entered pack territory, and the rest of him recognized her as you recognized a person who had been part of your frame of reference for a long time. She had been part of his Blackpine as the ridgelines were. Present. Unremarked on. Until she wasn't, and then the absence had a shape.

She came down from the step stool and turned.

His wolf hit the inside of his chest like a fist.

Mate. Ours. Now.

He had been expecting this. He had known this was coming. He had told himself he was prepared for this, that he could hold the wall through one normal interaction, that he was a man who had been managing himself under pressure for thirty-one years, and this wasn't different.

He wasn't prepared.

She looked at him with the brown eyes he remembered from summers, her recognition landing a half-second before he'd seen it in her face. Not alarmed. Assessing. The nurse looked, the one who took a quick inventory and drew rapid conclusions.

"Hi," she said. "Can I help you?"

"Batteries," he said. His voice came out lower than he intended, rougher. His wolf was settling into his chest like ballast. "I need, yeah. Batteries."

"Aisle three," she said. "Far end, left side."

He went to aisle three.

He stood in front of the battery display for approximately fifteen seconds. His wolf wasn't helping. His wolf was radiating a quality that could only be described as smug, which was deeply unhelpful given the circumstances. He reached for the first box his hand found. C-cell. He didn't need C-cell batteries. He didn't have a single device in his cabin that required C-cell batteries. He took two boxes and went back to the counter.

She was already behind the register, waiting with practiced retail patience. She looked at the two boxes without expression. He could feel her making the same calculation he had just made, reaching the same conclusion about the C-cell batteries.

"Six forty-two," she said.

He put a twenty on the counter.

Progress, his wolf said.

This isn't progress. This is a transaction. This is me buying batteries I don't need, he thought back.

"Do you want change?"

"Keep it." He was already turning toward the door because if he stood at this counter for one more second, he was going to say words he hadn't planned, words that came from his wolf rather than from the calculation he had made about controlled contact and holding the wall. "For the—put it toward the store."

He went through the door.

The bell shrieked behind him.

HE SAT in his truck for two minutes before he started the engine.

His wolf was insufferable. It had been insufferable since the moment she turned toward him and was showing no signs of becoming less insufferable. *Ours,* it said, with the absolute certainty of a creature that had never doubted this at all. *She is here. She knows. She noticed.*

She noticed because I was obvious, Jace thought back.

Good.

He pulled out onto Main Street. The cold was dry and clear, the mountains white above the tree line, October doing what October did in Montana, arriving with purpose.

He drove.

The memory came as it always came, not as a flashback but as a fact he carried, the pressure of it as present as an old injury, not acute but real. A woman he had met on a trail outside Glacier, six years after he and Cole had taken over running BWR together, when he had still been learning the loneliness of being Beta and thinking that maybe it was all right to let someone in. She had been warm and easy to talk to and she had made him feel, for a few months, like the wall was a barrier he had built unnecessarily.

He had told her what she would be to him. Not just what he was; the species, the biology, the fact of the pack, but what the bond meant. What he needed. What it would ask of her life if she said yes. He had handed it to her whole, on a trail, with the confidence of a man who thought she was ready because she had seemed happy, and happiness would absorb the impact. It hadn't. The word she used, monster.

The voice she used, flat with a terror that had curdled into disgust. She had moved to Florida within the month. He hadn't heard from her since, and he hadn't let anyone close since, and the wall he had rebuilt was designed so that he would never have to hear that word in that voice again.

For six years, he had mastered the art of the wall, understood its boundaries, and remained safely within them. He had cultivated warmth and ease, connecting effortlessly with everyone in Blackpine and any woman who happened to linger near him, all while ensuring that he revealed nothing of true importance.

He turned onto the forest road toward his cabin.

Lily Thornton wasn't Amanda.

This wasn't his wolf talking. His wolf had many opinions, and most of them were about proximity and possession and the word *ours*, and they weren't always the opinions of a creature with full context. But on this point, his wolf was right in a way that Jace could articulate with his own reasoning, Lily Thornton had grown up in a family that had known what the Mercers were for three generations. She wasn't someone who had stumbled into the secret from outside. She had grown up adjacent to it, in the same town, in the same inner circle that had always understood the essential strangeness of Blackpine and kept it. She wasn't going to look at him as Amanda had looked at him.

He didn't know what she was going to do.

You know exactly what she's going to do, his wolf pressed.

He didn't argue. He wanted to argue and couldn't quite get there.

The cabin came into view through the pines, the one he had built in the year after Amanda, because he had needed to work . He had taken six months to build it, slow and precise, measuring twice and cutting once, fitting every joint as his father had taught him before his father died. It was a good cabin. It was what he had made with his hands when trust and hope had proved themselves forces that could break.

He sat in the truck for a while after he turned off the engine.

He hadn't let himself go to the store. He had told himself he was giving her time to settle in, that she had come for Dottie and not for him, that the Thornton family's knowledge of the pack's nature didn't mean Lily personally wanted to be handed this particular information right now. All of this was true. It was also true that he had been afraid.

He wasn't afraid anymore.

As he sat in his truck outside the cabin, the October

chill seeped in, and two boxes of batteries sat uselessly beside him.

He hadn't been resolved since before Amanda. He hadn't known he was building toward it until it arrived, and it had arrived the moment Lily Thornton turned on a step stool and looked at him like she was already filing the data.

She was going to figure out what he was. That was the honest assessment. She had grown up adjacent to the truth. She was a woman who noticed patterns and drew accurate conclusions, and she was now in Blackpine running a store alongside people who were bad at hiding what they were to anyone paying close attention. She was going to figure it out whether he told her or not.

He would rather she learn it from him.

He tested the thought the way he tested anything load-bearing, and it held. Since Amanda, he hadn't once thought, I would rather she knew. Instead, he had assumed that no one could know. He believed he wouldn't put anyone through that experience again, neither himself nor them.

He had been reasonably good at it. The wall had been designed for strangers, people who came from outside and would leave when they understood what they'd found. It had served its purpose so well that he had stopped asking whether it was still the right tool.

Lily Thornton wasn't a stranger, and she wasn't going to leave, not as Amanda had left, because she wasn't Amanda and this wasn't the same situation.

He would rather she knew. That was the truth. He

didn't know how to tell her yet, or when, or what the words were, but the impulse was real and it was his, not his wolf's.

His wolf said nothing. It was the silence of a creature watching someone arrive at a conclusion it had held since that first day in the store.

Jace got out of the truck and went inside.

He put the C-cell batteries in the drawer with the others.

Cole was at HQ when Jace arrived the following morning, already at the map table with a mug of coffee and the expression of a man who had been up since before the sun and had made peace with this.

He glanced up. "You went in."

It wasn't a question. Cole's read on his pack's emotional state wasn't a skill Jace had ever been able to fully account for; it was part of being Alpha, how certain frequencies came through the bond that were too quiet for the individual members to hear but not for the one who held the center. Or possibly Cole had known Jace his while life, had been watching him avoid the general store, and had drawn the conclusion that any person with working eyes would.

"I went in," Jace said.

Cole turned back to the map table. He picked up his coffee, drank from it, and didn't say anything else.

His brother could have said *it's about time*, or *I told you so,* or any of several truths that were entirely accurate and would have landed wrong. He said nothing, and in the nothing there was *I saw you. I'm glad. We don't have to talk about it.*

Jace got himself a coffee and sat across the map table, and they went over the trail reports for the northern sector, and the morning proceeded as mornings proceeded, and his wolf was quiet with the settled patience of a creature that had gotten what it wanted and was content to wait for the rest.

THREE

BROTHER'S KEEPER

The trail reports for the northern sector took an hour and a half—longer than it should have. Jace was aware that he had read the same stretch of the northern boundary three times and retained approximately none of it, and that Cole was aware of this too, and had chosen not to comment on it. He appreciated the choice. He read the northern boundary a fourth time, and this time some of the information landed.

When they were done, Cole rolled up the maps efficiently and said, without looking up, "Harper's making dinner tonight. Seven o'clock. Pack dinner, not only us."

"I'll be there."

Cole picked up both mugs and went toward the kitchen. At the doorway, he stopped. "She's going to be in Blackpine for a while," he said. Not Lily's name. Just *she*. They both knew who he meant. "Dottie's ahead of schedule, but that puts her here through at least January."

"I know."

"You've got time," Cole said. *Don't slow down. Don't be careless. Time exists. Use it.* He went into the kitchen.

Jace sat with the rolled maps and thought about January.

Three months. Three months wasn't long when you had spent six years telling yourself the wall was permanent.

That was the real problem, and he was clear-eyed enough to name it, not the time, not the approach, not the question of when. The wall itself. The ease with which he had been performing since Amanda, the version of himself that connected with everyone in Blackpine and disclosed nothing of weight. That version wasn't going to work with Lily Thornton. She had been filing data on him since the first day in the store. He would rather she built it from something real.

Or you could tell her, his wolf rumbled.

He got up and refiled the maps.

REID WAS in the equipment room when Jace came through to check the rope inventory. The pack's tracker at the workbench, a carabiner in his hands and a tool that required concentration. He occupied space unobtrusively yet completely.

He glanced up when Jace came in and looked back down without speaking. This was normal.

Jace pulled the rope inventory sheet and started checking against what was racked. He had done this inventory three days ago. He did it again now because it needed to be done and also because standing in the equipment room doing useful work felt better than sitting in the trail report room not reading trail reports.

After a while Reid said, "She's a nurse."

Jace kept his eyes on the inventory sheet. "Yes."

"Spent six years in Bozeman. Trauma unit." Reid said it the same way he said everything, as a confirmed fact from a reliable source "Her grandmother told Nora. Nora told me."

"I'm aware."

"People who work trauma units," Reid said, focused on the carabiner, "are generally good at staying functional when reality doesn't match what they expected."

Jace looked at him.

Reid didn't look up from the carabiner. "Just an observation," he said.

Jace went back to the rope inventory. His wolf was quiet as it got quiet when a voice from outside confirmed what it had been saying from inside. He checked off the last rope on the sheet, filed the inventory, and went back to work.

He didn't ask Reid how he knew what he was asking. Reid always knew. It was one of the more useful and occasionally frustrating aspects of him.

He spent the rest of the morning on maintenance tasks that required his hands but not much of his mind, which was what he needed because his mind was running the same problem from different angles and arriving at the same answer each time; he was going to have to be careful. Not avoidant; he had tried avoidance, like driving past the store and buying hardware he didn't need. Careful. Present but paced. Let her see who he was before he told her what he was. Give her room to form her own assessment.

His wolf found this plan deeply tedious and communicated this clearly.

I understand, Jace thought at it. *We're doing it anyway.*

He drove back through town at lunch to pick up a part for one of the ATVs from the hardware store and passed the general store without slowing. He noted the OPEN sign in the window. He noted the light inside. He didn't stop.

He was being careful.

He was also, his wolf pointed out with unhelpful accuracy, watching her.

SATURDAY MORNING, the store was quiet until nine.

Lily had been awake since six. In the kitchen above the store, she made coffee and stood at the window looking down at the street. A truck she hadn't seen before turned off Main Street, heading toward the mountains, and her thoughts followed it. She had told herself she wasn't thinking about Jace Mercer. She was.

She applied what she had.

Data: Jace Mercer had walked into the store on Friday, bought the wrong batteries, overpaid by thirteen dollars and fifty-eight cents, and left before she could return his change.

Data: he had known she would be there. She had been certain of this the moment she turned and saw his face, and she was certain of it this morning. That wasn't the expression of a man who had been surprised.

Data: according to Earl, he had remembered her during the holidays when she'd come back. According to Mrs. Patterson, the Mercers were original stock, the inner circle, part of the essential fabric of Blackpine in ways her grandparents had acknowledged but never explained.

Data: She had grown up in a house where the Mercers were referenced with a sense of deference that her grandparents never explained to her directly. She had left at eighteen before the explanation was offered, if it had been going to be offered.

She poured a second cup of coffee and went down to the inventory she had started the day before.

THE MORNING REGULARS arrived as usual. Mr. Hendricks for hardware supplies. A woman Lily didn't recognize, who bought three tins of coffee and made brief conversation about the weather, which was getting colder as Montana autumn settled in for good.

Dottie came downstairs at ten, moving with the careful precision of a woman who had been told not to rush.

"You're hovering again," she said.

"I'm watching you navigate the stairs," Lily said it without looking up from the delivery manifest. "There's a difference."

"The stairs are fine. The doctor said the stairs were fine."

"The doctor said the stairs were fine with the handrail."

Dottie used the handrail with the air of a woman doing this under protest and arrived at the bottom with her dignity intact. She looked around the store, assessed the reorganization Lily had done to the front shelves, and reached a verdict of acceptable.

"Earl's at the hardware store," she said. "He'll be back by noon."

"I know. He told me."

Dottie moved unhurried to the cast-iron stove and added a log from the basket beside it. The stove was original to the building, Earl had told her, which in Blackpine terms meant it predated the county's formal record-keeping. Lily had spent twenty minutes on her first morning making sure she understood its particular requirements before she trusted herself with it.

"You're thinking about the Mercers again," Dottie said.

Lily looked up. "Am I that obvious?"

"You get a certain quality when you're working through a problem." Dottie settled into the chair she kept behind the counter, the one that had been behind the counter for as long as Lily could remember. "You did it as a child, too. Your face goes very still."

"I'm a nurse. Still faces are useful."

"Mm." Dottie's *mm* was the one that meant, *that's true and also not the whole picture.* "Ask me what you're going to ask me."

Lily put down the manifest. "What did you know about the Mercers? When I was growing up."

Dottie was quiet. Not uncertain quiet, but deciding-how-much-to-give quiet. "Enough," she said. "More than we ever told you."

"Why didn't you tell me?"

"You were young. And then you left." She said it without accusation, just the fact of it. "The conversation requires a certain amount of context to land correctly, and the context was easier to provide if you were here. You weren't here."

Lily thought about this. Eight years was a long time to be not here. "And now?"

Dottie looked at her with the eyes that saw the truth behind the surface. "Now you're back," she said. "And Jace Mercer came in yesterday and bought the wrong batteries." Her expression was that of a woman who found this development both unsurprising and privately satisfying. "The context will present itself."

"That's not an answer."

"No," Dottie agreed. "It's not." She picked up her book from behind the counter and opened it to her place. "Some truths need to be learned, not told. You'll understand the difference when you get there."

Lily looked at her grandmother, at the steel-gray hair and the cardigan and the sharp comfortable certainty of a woman who had been living with this knowledge for decades and had made peace with what it required of her.

She picked up the manifest.

She would be patient. She was good at patient. She could wait.

She'd begun building the list in her head. The facts she knew, the facts she'd been told, and the gaps between them. It was the same list she'd started building the night before, lying in her childhood bedroom with the ceiling above her and the Blackpine silence outside, a silence that wasn't empty but full of secrets the town kept to itself.

She had data. She needed more. She would get more.

Outside, the October cold lay against the window glass. The mountains were white at the top and the trees were going gold and the light at this altitude, the angle through the pines, was a quality Bozeman had never had. She had forgotten this. She had forgotten, or let herself forget, that Blackpine had a beauty that was its own, that she had spent eight years telling herself she didn't miss.

MARGE HOLLISTER CAME in at half past eleven.

Lily had met Marge briefly the summer she was sixteen, remembered her as the woman who ran the Summit Diner with a combination of warmth and efficiency that made it the center of Blackpine social life. She had the same solid presence, the same apron she wore everywhere, the eyes that took in a room and cataloged it in a single sweep.

She bought a bag of flour and a tin of baking powder and set them on the counter and then didn't immediately move toward the door. Lily had been in Blackpine long enough to recognize this pattern.

"Settling in?" Marge asked.

"Getting there."

"Good." Marge looked around the store, took in the reorganized shelves, and kept whatever she thought about them to herself. "Your grandmother says you're a good nurse."

"I'm out of practice." Eight months was long enough to matter, at least to her confidence.

"You'll get it back." She said it like a fact. "Things do."

She was building toward a point. Lily waited.

"Jace Mercer," Marge said, with the directness of a woman who had decided not to approach her subject sideways. "Good man. Had a hard few years, back around when he and Cole were first getting the rescue operation running properly." She picked up the flour and the baking powder and settled her bag on her shoulder. "He doesn't talk about it much. But he's better than he was. I thought you should know, since you've been friendly before."

Lily looked at her. "Is that the whole story?"

Marge's mouth turned up at one corner in a way that suggested she found this question either funny or exactly what she expected. "Not even close," she said. "But it's what I'm telling you today." She moved toward the door. "Come by the diner sometime. The huckleberry pie is the same as it always was."

The bell shrieked behind her.

Lily stood at the register.

He's better than he was. A hard few years. Whatever had happened to Jace Mercer, it was part of the general architecture of secrets in this town that people knew but didn't hand over directly. She had been offered a corner of it. She tucked the corner away and kept going.

The afternoon came in with a bank of clouds moving off the mountains, the temperature dropping as the season meant it would. Lily restocked the upper shelves from the morning delivery, helped Mr. Hendricks find the gauge of wire he needed for a fence repair, and answered three phone calls for Earl that she handled by writing careful messages in the notebook beside the register.

She was, she thought, unreasonably glad to be here.

She had told herself she was coming for Dottie. She had told herself it was temporary. She hadn't told herself how much she had missed a town that was sure of itself, that knew what it was, that didn't require you to perform anything in order to belong to it.

She wasn't thinking about Bozeman.

She went back to work. She made a note in the margin of the manifest.

Ask Earl about the Mercer family. When the time is right.

She looked at the note and then added, below it.

What is the right time?

She didn't have an answer for that yet. She crossed out the second line and kept the first.

Outside, the October cold had moved in properly. The pines along the road held their stillness. Blackpine at late afternoon had its own quality. How the light fell when the mountains to the west had already taken the sun and the sky was still bright. An in-between hour, neither afternoon nor evening, an hour the town had been keeping its own counsel through for longer than anyone living could remember.

FOUR

SMALL TOWN EYES

By the end of the first week, Lily had rebuilt the inventory system, reorganized the front shelves by frequency of use rather than supplier category, and established a morning routine that involved coffee at six, the delivery manifest by seven, and Mrs. Patterson at eight-fifteen.

Mrs. Patterson arrived with her supplement printout on Tuesday, her opinions about Lily's sleep schedule on Wednesday, and a friend on Thursday, who turned out to have opinions about altitude adjustment that were largely identical to Mrs. Patterson's, suggesting they had prepared for this together. Lily listened to all of it with the attention she brought to everything, noted the useful parts, thanked them, and they left satisfied, which was the important part.

The work itself wasn't difficult. She had grown up in this store every summer, knew its rhythms, and had understood since she was twelve that the general store ran on relationship as much as transaction. People came in for a box of nails and stayed for twenty minutes. People called to ask if Earl had an item in stock and ended up discussing a neighbor's health or the weather for fifteen minutes before getting to the actual question. She had watched Earl operate this way for her entire childhood and had absorbed more of it than she'd realized, because she was repeating the same behaviors without thinking, remembering names after one introduction, asking follow-up questions, holding the door for the person who was clearly heading out.

She was, she thought on Thursday afternoon, genuinely glad to be doing this.

This wasn't what she had expected to think. She had called it a pause. A placeholder while she figured out what came next.

It was possible she had been wrong about that.

DOTTIE WAS DOWNSTAIRS MORE each day, making tea at the kitchen table in the morning, appearing behind the counter in the afternoons with a book and her observant stillness. The doctor had been right about her being ahead of schedule. By Thursday, she was moving through the store without the careful precision of the first few days, settling back into familiar ease, her feet knowing every board in the floor.

"Stop watching me," she said to Lily on Thursday afternoon without looking up from her book.

"I'm stocking the vitamin shelf."

"You've been stocking the same three bottles for ten minutes."

Lily moved to the next shelf. "You're doing well."

"I know I am." Dottie turned a page. "I told you I would." She turned a page. The certainty of seventy years required no commentary. "Earl told me you reorganized the inventory system."

"It needed it."

"He's been threatening to for twenty years." The corner of Dottie's mouth turned up. "He'll never admit you did it better."

"He won't have to."

Dottie looked at her over the top of her book with the expression that meant, *that's exactly right, and also I like you.* She went back to reading.

Nora Callahan came in on Wednesday.

Lily had seen her briefly the summer she was fifteen, retained a vague impression of a woman who managed operations, and not much else. In person, Nora was more defined than that impression, late forties, gray-streaked hair pulled back, quiet authority that held a room's center without appearing to take up space. She moved through the store with familiar ease and picked up two tins of coffee, a bag of rice, and brought them to the counter.

"Nora Callahan," she said, as though Lily might not know. "I run operations at Blackpine Wilderness Rescue."

"Lily Thornton."

"I know." Nora set the items on the counter. "Earl told me you were coming. Dottie told me before that." She set the items on the counter. "How are you finding it?"

"The store runs itself mostly. I'm learning the rhythms."

"Good." Nora glanced around the store, making a brief assessment as someone taking stock. "I hear you were in emergency medicine in Bozeman."

"Six years. Trauma unit."

Nora nodded once. "That's useful," she said. "Good to have someone like that in Blackpine. We take care of our own here. Earl's family is our family. That makes you ours."

She paid for the coffee and the rice and moved toward the door efficiently, message delivered, other business waiting.

"Come by BWR sometime," she said. "Harper would like to see you. She's been in Blackpine long enough now that she always wants to meet anyone with roots here."

The bell announced her departure.

Lily stood at the counter with the money in the till and thought about how *we take care of our own here*. It wasn't the first time she had heard that sentiment, but how Nora said it was different from how most people said phrases like that. Not a pleasantry. A fact.

She noted it.

∾

S HE SAW Jace twice that week.

Once on Tuesday, across Main Street, talking to a man she didn't recognize, the posture of someone mid-explanation, hands moving. He didn't look toward the store. She wasn't watching for him.

Once on Thursday, through the window, the BWR truck idled at the hardware store down the street. She watched until he came out, noted the direction he went, and turned back to the inventory sheet.

Earl noticed. He said nothing.

She added his name to the manifest note below Ask Earl about the Mercer family. When the time is right. Jace Mercer. She looked at the list and turned the page.

S HE ASKED Earl about the Mercers on Thursday evening, he was closing the register, and she was sweeping the floor near the door, and the moment felt as good as any, which was what she had learned about asking Earl questions, you didn't schedule them, you waited for them to arrive in the natural flow of a quiet moment.

"The Mercers," she said. "They've been here a long time."

"Yes," Earl said.

"Longer than most families."

"Mm." He closed the register drawer. The *mm* was the one that meant, *I am listening to your question and I am also deciding how to answer it.*

"They own a lot of land out past the facility."

"They do."

"And the BWR operation, Cole runs it, Jace is second." She kept her voice matter-of-fact. "The whole town knows them."

"The whole town does."

She swept the last of the dust into the dustpan and looked up at him. "Are you going to tell me anything?"

Earl regarded her with the weathered patience of a man who had been considering how to answer this question since before she arrived. "When it's time," he said. "Not before."

"That's Dottie's answer."

"She married me for a reason." He put the deposit bag on the shelf for the morning run and looked at her with eyes that weren't unkind. "You're asking the right questions. That's enough for now."

She put the broom away. She wasn't frustrated, exactly. She'd learned to wait for information to cohere on its own schedule. The Mercers were a question the town had been sitting with for a long time. She could sit with it a little longer.

Outside, the temperature had dropped sharply after dark. She could hear the wind off the mountains through the gap at the bottom of the door, a high keening sound that meant the weather was changing seriously. Earl had mentioned the forecast the day before, a low-pressure system moving in from the northwest. Montana autumn didn't make gradual announcements.

She went upstairs and found Dottie at the kitchen

table with tea and a look that said she had heard the conversation through the floor.

"He'll tell you," Dottie said. "When the time is right."

"Everyone keeps saying that."

"Because everyone means it." Dottie wrapped her hands around her mug. "The timing matters with some truths. This is one of those truths."

Lily made herself a cup of tea and sat across from her grandmother, looking out the window at the dark mountain line against the darker sky. The wind moved through the pines with weight. The first real cold of the season was coming, and it would come fast, as weather came fast here, as the mountains had always operated, not gradually but absolutely, a full commitment to whatever they were doing.

She was, she realized, not actually thinking about leaving.

She hadn't thought about Bozeman since Tuesday.

Frank called on Friday.

She had been expecting it. Her father called every Friday from Billings, had done this since she moved to Bozeman, and the calls were usually brief, *how are you, how's the work, how's Dottie.* She answered them in order, and he responded with *good, good, good,* and they discussed nothing in particular for seven minutes and hung up.

This call was different.

After she had answered the first three questions in order, he skipped the pause. "I've been reading about that family. The Mercers."

Lily set down the delivery slip she'd been holding. "Why?"

"Because you're in Blackpine and they run most of what happens in Blackpine." He'd been thinking about this for longer than the current week. She could hear it. "That rescue outfit they run. The land they own, some of that goes back further than the town's official records. Did you know that?"

"I didn't know you were looking into property records."

"I've been doing some reading." He said it as her father said statements when he wanted to minimize how much effort the research had required. He had been a county assessor for nineteen years, and he had a practiced patience for public records. "There's a land trust connected to them that predates the county by about fifteen years. That's unusual."

"Dad."

"I'm not saying anything. I'm just telling you what I found." A pause. "The town's got a lot of history with that family. Old history. Some of the town records from the 1970s reference them in the context of what the county called a *community stewardship arrangement,* which isn't a standard legal designation."

"I don't know what that means."

"Neither does the county, apparently. The notation just exists." Another pause. "I want you to be careful."

She understood what he was asking, which wasn't what he was saying. He was asking her to be careful around the Mercers, which meant he had concerns about them that went beyond normal protective paternal interest. She didn't know what had generated that concern. She didn't know how long he had been carrying it.

"I'm fine," she said. "I'm running Earl's store. Nothing is happening."

"Good. Call me if anything seems off."

"I will."

She hung up, stood with the phone in her hand, and looked at the October light coming through the store window, golden and low, the low angle of late afternoon in the mountains. Outside, the temperature had dropped a few more degrees since morning. The season was making itself permanent.

She added this to the list in the margin of the manifest. She had data, and she had gaps, and she had the patience of a woman who had spent years in the ER learning that the answer you were waiting to understand would come into focus when it was ready, not before.

She turned the page.

The rest of the afternoon was quiet. Mrs. Kowalski came in for flour and stayed to tell Lily about the winter two years ago when the pass had been closed for eleven days, which was a record, and to recommend that Lily acquire a particular brand of thermal underlayer before November arrived, which it was going to do without apology. Lily wrote down the brand.

Earl returned from a late errand and put the coffee on

without mentioning it. By the end of the first week she had understood this was the shape of the close of day with him, not conversation, not ceremony, the coffee appearing and the mug handed over. She took it.

Outside, the light had gone flat. The mountains were gone into an overcast that had been building since midafternoon, the dense uniform gray of a system moving in rather than passing through. The water tower at the edge of town kept its three-degree lean in the gray the same way it kept it in clear sky, without registering the difference.

Her father thought the Mercer family was strange. He wasn't wrong. He had a county assessor's instinct for anomalies in the public record, and he had been running it against Blackpine's records, which meant he had been thinking about this since Dottie's stroke. She didn't know what he thought he was protecting her from. She did know that he protected obliquely, kept his worry at a factual distance, and expressed concern through data rather than directly. She recognized this because she did the same.

She drank her coffee, watched the gray sky, and thought about the community stewardship arrangement, the land trust, and the property records that predated the county, and everything else she had been adding to the list she was building in the margins of the manifest and in the back of her mind since last Friday, when Jace Mercer had walked through the door with a look on his face that wasn't surprise.

She had been here for seven days.

She had told herself she'd drive back in January, provisional on Dottie's recovery. Dottie was recovering ahead of schedule. January was looking more possible than it had.

She wasn't thinking about January.

She finished the coffee, washed the mug, and put it back in the cabinet where it lived, and went upstairs to start dinner, and the first snow of October began to fall outside the window in small, serious flakes, the weather having made up its mind.

FIVE

THE CATCH

The first snow had left a quarter inch on the steps overnight and a thin sheet of ice underneath it where the melt had refrozen before morning.

Lily had noted this when she came down at six-fifteen to open the store. She had put on her coat and gone to the back to find the bag of rock salt, only to discover it was behind three boxes of stock that had come in on Friday and had not yet been shelved. The Saturday delivery had been left on the front landing. She would bring that in first and come back for the salt.

This was how she ended up carrying the first box out through the front door at eight-forty on a Saturday morning when the ice was on the steps, and the rock salt was in the back.

The box was heavy. She had misjudged the weight distribution because she had been holding it with the manifest in her other hand, and the manifest slipped as she came through the door. She reached for it automatically, and her left foot went off the edge of the top step onto the ice.

She didn't fall.

Hands on her arms, two of them, firm and immediate, catching her weight before she had fully processed that she was going down. She felt the contact through her coat, the grip steady and sure, and her looked up to who had helped her.

Jace Mercer.

His hands were on both her upper arms. He was looking at her with the expression she had learned in two weeks to recognize, the one underneath his usual ease that came through when he hadn't had time to arrange his face. Alert and focused and intense in a way she didn't yet have a name for.

"You okay?" he asked.

"Ice." She heard how flat that sounded and added, "Yes. Thank you."

He didn't release her immediately. His hands were hot through the layers of her coat. Not just body heat. Hot in a way her nurse's brain cataloged as elevated body temperature. *Not a fever. This is different.*

She became aware that she hadn't moved away.

He let go. She stepped back and looked down at the box she had kept hold of through all of this, and then at the steps, and then at the door.

"I was going to salt those," she said.

"I'll do it." He picked up the manifest she had dropped, which had gone three steps down, and held it out to her. "Where's the salt?"

"Behind the stock in the back."

"I'll get it."

She started to say she could do it. He was already past her and through the door, moving through the store with familiar ease. He had grown up knowing Earl. He would know where the back room was.

She stood on the top step with the heavy box and the October cold and her heartbeat, which was doing work she was going to attribute entirely to the near-fall and not to the heat of his hands through her coat, because that was the reasonable attribution.

He came back with the salt. She stepped aside. He did the steps methodically, all three of them and the landing at the bottom, practiced and thorough, a thin coat doing more harm than a thick one. When he was done, he straightened and looked at her.

"You should have done those before you came out."

"I was planning to."

"The steps were icy."

"I noticed." She set the box down on the cleared landing. "I was getting the salt."

A flicker of amusement moved through his expression, briefly, before his face settled back into neutrality. "I know," he said. "I'm not—" He stopped. "I know."

She studied him, the BWR jacket, and the sandy hair and the careful stillness of a man who had been about to finish a sentence and had chosen not to. She had been noting details about Jace Mercer for two weeks. The list was getting long.

"Were you coming in?" she asked.

"I had a question for Earl about the delivery schedule. The Thursday run sometimes conflicts with our morning training."

She studied him. "Earl's not here on Saturday mornings. He does the bank run."

"Right." His stare dropped to the steps. "I knew that."

She picked up the box. "Aisle three. Same place," she said. "If you need batteries."

The corner of his mouth moved. Not a full smile. The gesture of one, contained. "I'm good on batteries," he said. "For a while."

She went inside with the box. She heard him behind her on the salted steps, and then the bell, and then his footsteps on the wooden floor.

She carried the box down to the back room, set it down, and stood with her hands on the top of it. The heat of his hands through her coat had been notable. She filed it.

She went back out front. He was looking at the display near the counter, the reorganized one, the frequency-of-use layout she had done on her second day. He had a tin of coffee.

She glanced at the coffee then at him. He met her eyes.

"Three fifty," she said.

He put four dollars on the counter.

This was better, she thought, than last time. Last time he had overpaid by thirteen dollars and fifty-eight cents and left without change. This time, the amount was correct, and he stayed through the transaction. Progress, of a sort.

She gave him his fifty cents. He took it without comment.

The store was quiet around them. The cast-iron stove ticked in the corner. She had learned its rhythm over the past two weeks, the tick of expanding metal when Earl added a log, the sound of the damper, and how the heat moved through the small space in the mornings before it warmed enough to open the front door. She knew the boards that creaked near the hardware section. She knew the light at this hour, the low October angle that came through the window and hit the shelves at the back, making the whole store look like a scene out of a photograph from fifty years ago.

She hadn't expected to like it here so much.

"The steps should hold," he said.

"Thank you for doing them."

"They needed it."

She had the distinct sense that they were both waiting to see which of them would speak next and what would be said when one of them did.

HE HADN'T BEEN PLANNING to stop at the store.

He had been on his way back from checking the trailhead cameras on the east side of pack territory, which took him through town on the mountain road, past the end of Main Street, where the general store wasn't, though it was in the vicinity. He had told himself he wasn't going to stop. He had driven past the end of Main Street, seen the OPEN sign in the store window, and thought about the Thursday delivery conflict with morning training, a real issue he had been meaning to ask Earl about for two weeks. He had turned the truck around.

He wasn't, his wolf observed, getting better at the *not-avoidant but careful* strategy he had established.

He had been parking when she came out the front door.

His wolf had moved him before his conscious mind had finished processing what was happening; she was going down, the steps were covered with ice, and he was across the sidewalk with his hands on her arms before he had decided to do any of that. His wolf had a clear opinion about Lily Thornton falling and the opinion was no.Her eyes found his.

He had her weight. Her arms under his hands, even through the coat, and the heat of her as he had started to understand temperature differently in the nine days since she had come back, not as a metaphor but as information, the pack's elevated temperature reading against her ordinary temperature, a difference he felt in his palms and wrists and the whole system of him.

She looked at him with the expression he had come to know as her assessing one, the one that was cataloging.

He let go. He bent down for the manifest. He offered it to her and went inside for the salt.

He did the steps. She stood on the landing, and he wasn't thinking about the heat he had felt through her coat, or how she hadn't pulled away immediately, or how she had looked at him when he came back outside to do the steps with the expression of someone adding a fact to a list they were keeping.

She knew events were unfolding. He had known this since Friday when she turned around. She had been building this one for two weeks.

Good, his wolf said.

Not yet, Jace thought back.

He had told Amanda badly, what she would be to him, what the bond would ask of her life, what he needed from her, on a trail in the middle of a moment that had felt right because she had been laughing and the light had been good, with no preparation and no context for what he was about to put in her hands. He wasn't going to do it that way again.

When she came back inside with the box, he had done the lower steps. She set it down on the landing and looked at him with a question; he could see her deciding whether to ask.

"Were you coming in?" she asked.

"I had a question for Earl about the delivery schedule."

She told him Earl wasn't here on Saturday mornings. He knew that. He had always known that. She knew that he knew that. He could tell by how she said it.

He had nothing. His attention dropped to the steps because they were safer than her face.

"I'm good on batteries," he said, when she offered him the option. "For a while."

She went inside. He followed. She moved through the store to the back to shelve whatever was in the box, and he stayed near the front, looking at the display near the counter that had been reorganized since his last visit, the frequency-of-use layout that Reid had mentioned Nora had mentioned to him, the Blackpine information network working as it always did. He picked up a tin of coffee he didn't need.

She returned, moving with the efficient, unhurried nature that was one of the traits he had been noticing about her for two weeks. Her eyes fell on the coffee in his hand.

"Three fifty," she said.

He put four dollars on the counter. She gave him fifty cents back, which was the correct change. He took it. They were both aware that this was an improvement on the last transaction.

"The steps should hold," he said.

"Thank you for doing them."

"They needed it."

He had ten seconds, he thought, before one of them spoke words to end this or Earl came back from the bank or the bell announced someone coming in.

"I owe you an explanation," he said. He hadn't planned to say it.

She went still as she went still when she was paying close attention. "For what?"

"For, how I was. When I came in. The first time." He held the tin of coffee. "I was strange. I know I was strange. I've been thinking about how to explain it."

"You don't have to."

"I want to." He said it before he could reconsider it. "I just don't, I need to do it right. When I do it."

She watched him, and he could feel her processing this, the nurse's mind running its analysis, deciding how much to push and what to wait for.

"Okay," she said.

Just that. *Okay.* Not *when* or *why* or *what is it.* Just, *I heard you. I'll wait.*

He said goodbye, went through the door, heard the bell shriek behind him, and stood on the salted steps in the cold before he went to his truck. His wolf was doing several operations at once, all of them variations on *"see ours and good."* He let it. He had earned nothing yet. But the door was in the wall now, and he had put it there himself, and she had said *okay,* and that was progress.

He drove home with the coffee he didn't need and thought that January was a long time and also not long enough and that he was going to have to figure out how to do this right.

Earl came back from the bank at nine-fifteen.

Lily had been behind the counter since Jace left, running the morning receipts with a focus she was applying more deliberately than usual.

"Steps are done," she told Earl when he came in.

"Good." He stamped his feet on the mat. "Ice?"

"Overnight refreeze. Jace Mercer did the salting."

Earl said nothing for three seconds. This was notable because Earl was a man who had a response to almost everything, even if it was only an mm. Three seconds of silence from Earl meant he was considering what kind of silence was appropriate.

"Good man," he said, and went to hang up his coat.

She went back to the receipts.

What Jace had said sat in her mind like a fact she was choosing not to look at directly. *I owe you an explanation. I need to do it right.*

She added it to the list in her head, which was getting crowded.

She turned the page on the receipts and started on the Friday stack and told herself she wasn't thinking about the heat of his hands, which was true in the same way that telling herself she wasn't thinking about Bozeman was true.

Outside, the snow from the night before was still on the rooftops, the mountains white and clear above it, the sky the hard bright blue that came after the first snow, that particular color that Blackpine had and Bozeman didn't, the color of altitude and cold and the clarity that came when the weather had done what it came to do and was finished.

She was here for Dottie.

She was also beginning to understand that she was here for a reason that she didn't have the words for yet.

SIX

THE CHARMER'S MASK

The Friday pack dinner had been going on since before their father died.

Nora had started it, which was characteristic of Nora, she saw that a pack without a center would drift apart, and she built a center, and the center was food on Friday evenings, and everyone present who wasn't on a call-out. The tradition had survived Cole's first terrible year as Alpha, their mother's illness, and the long stretch of years when the pack had been smaller, quieter, and less certain of itself than it was now. You kept it not because the impulse was always there, but because the alternative was losing a structure that was load-bearing.

This was the truth about load-bearing rituals. You understood their weight most clearly in the years when they were hardest to maintain. The year after their father died, Cole had almost canceled it twice. Nora hadn't let him. In retrospect, the fact that she hadn't let him was the reason the pack had stayed a pack through those years, rather than becoming a collection of individuals who happened to share territory and a professional cover story. The dinner wasn't about the food. It was about you showing up.

Jace arrived at quarter to seven and found Harper in the kitchen helping Nora, a development that had occurred sometime in the last several months and had become, without announcement, a fixture. Harper Stone had come to Blackpine as an investigative journalist with a story to kill and had ended up being the pack's best argument that human mates weren't a liability but a structural improvement. She had been here eight months. She moved through the pack HQ without announcing herself and without looking like she was working not to.

Jace found Cole in the living room, going over data on his tablet, and sat across from him.

"Problem?" Jace asked.

"Trail camera on the north boundary is offline again. Third time this month." Cole didn't look up. "Reid's going out tomorrow."

"The angle?"

"Camera three, northwest. Could be wind damage. Could be someone moving it." He turned the tablet so Jace could see the coverage gap the missing camera created. "Nothing critical. I want eyes on it."

Jace looked at the gap. The northern boundary had been quiet all autumn, with no significant intrusions and nothing that had triggered the pack bond in a concerning way. He had no reason to think the offline camera was anything more than an equipment failure. He also knew that Cole's read on territory anomalies was better than almost anyone's, and Cole had mentioned this camera three times in two weeks.

"I'll go with Reid tomorrow," Jace said.

Cole nodded and turned the tablet back and they sat in the comfortable silence of two people who had been working together long enough not to need to fill quiet with noise.

Danny arrived at seven with a bag of chips that Nora immediately confiscated for being the wrong kind and replaced it with a bowl of chips more acceptable. Danny accepted this with equanimity. Four years of the same exchange with Nora had stopped him from expecting a different outcome. He dropped into the armchair nearest the fire and looked at Jace with the expression of a twenty-six-year-old who had recently acquired a piece of information and was deciding how to deploy it.

This wasn't a subtle expression. Jace recognized it.

"So," Danny said.

"No," Jace said.

Danny grinned. "I didn't say anything."

"You were about to."

"I was making conversation." He took a chip from the bowl Nora had put in front of him.

From the far end of the room, Eli looked up from his phone. "Is she pretty?"

The room went briefly still. Cole didn't look up from his tablet. "The trail camera," he said.

Eli opened his mouth. "I was just—"

"The trail camera," Cole said again, with identical inflection.

Eli closed his mouth.

Danny ate a chip with the air of a man regretting that someone else had gotten there first. "I heard you've been in town a lot lately," he said to Jace, pivoting smoothly.

Cheerful innocence, absolutely no awareness of what he was doing. Danny said most things that way, which made it worse rather than better. "Earl's granddaughter seems nice. Really organized. She redid the whole inventory system in like two days."

"I know," Jace said.

"Apparently, she's a nurse? From Bozeman?" Danny helped himself to another chip. "You should come by more. Get to know her."

Jace looked at him. Danny's face was that of a man who genuinely didn't know why this comment had made everyone else in the room go still. Cole hadn't looked up from his tablet. Reid, who had appeared in the doorway from the kitchen at some point in the last twenty seconds, was studying the middle distance with extreme concentration.

"Sure," Jace said.

Danny ate the chip. "Cool," he said. "She seems—"

"Danny," Cole said, without looking up.

"Yeah?"

"The trail camera."

Danny's attention was redirected with the ease of a man whose attention was easily redirected. "Right, yeah. You said the northwest one? I've been thinking about that, actually, the angle on camera three has always been off, the mounting bracket was never right, maybe we—"

Jace got up and went to the kitchen.

Nora looked at him when he came in.

She handed him a knife and a cutting board with carrots on it without comment.

He cut carrots. She adjusted a pot on the stove. Harper had stepped out; voices in the other room suggested she had joined the trail camera conversation. The kitchen was quiet.

"She's settling in," Nora said eventually.

He cut another carrot. "I know."

"Dottie says she's not counting days anymore." She said it the same way she said most things as a piece of information being offered, not a point being pressed. "She was going to go back in January. She's not saying that anymore."

Jace didn't say anything.

"I told her the town takes care of its own," Nora said. "She filed it. She's been filing everything."

"She does that."

"She's a nurse. She looks at the available data and she waits for a pattern to emerge." Nora looked at him. "She's going to figure it out. You know that."

"I know."

"The question is whether she figures it out from you or from the town." She said it without judgment. "The town will tell her eventually. It's not a question of if. Blackpine's been keeping this secret for three generations of Thorntons, and every one of them was told at the right time. Lily is reaching the right time."

He put the cut carrots in the bowl she indicated. "I told her I owed her an explanation."

Nora was quiet. "What did she say?"

"She said okay."

Another pause. "And then?"

"And then nothing. She's waiting."

Nora looked at him with the expression she got when she thought a person was finally making the right choice after a long period of making it wrong. It was an expression he had been on the receiving end of once or twice in his life, usually after he had made a decision she had been quietly hoping he would make. "Good," she said.

He took the carrots to the table.

Before dinner, Reid pulled him aside near the equipment door.

"Camera three," he said.

"Cole told me. We're going out tomorrow."

"Right." Reid looked at him with the intensity he got when there was information he was deciding whether to share. He said it. "She came by the diner today."

Jace looked at him.

"I wasn't there. Marge told Nora. Lily stopped in for coffee late in the morning. Marge said she's been in a few times this week." He said it without inflection, the same way he reported trail conditions or weather patterns, information, no editorial. "Marge likes her."

"Most people like her."

"Marge likes her," Reid said. "Marge doesn't like most people. She likes the ones she's decided are going to stay."

He went back to the equipment room.

Jace stood in the hallway with that piece of information, thinking about Marge Hollister, who had lived in Blackpine for sixty-three years and had an accurate read on its people, which she deployed with surgical precision. He thought about what it meant that Marge had decided Lily Thornton was going to stay. He thought about the fact that Marge had been watching Blackpine long enough to notice when the patterns were shifting and had drawn her own conclusions with cheerful efficiency, matchmaking in this town since before Jace was born.

Good, his wolf said.

He went to join the others.

DINNER WAS the usual pack dinner, loud and relaxed, fueled by humor born from long-standing familiarity. Having worked and lived together long enough to know which stories would land and which ones would always be told wrong and become funnier made the atmosphere easygoing. Cole, even after eight months of watching Harper tend to his brother, was still surprised by Jace with his relaxed ease. The man who had carried the pack's weight alone for twelve years had, somewhere along the way, learned to laugh at jokes instead of merely managing tension.

Old Tom told the same story he had been telling since Jace was seventeen, about the time he had single-handedly resolved a territorial dispute with a grizzly by what Tom called strategic patience and what everyone else had eventually understood was Tom falling asleep in the bear's territory, with the bear deciding he wasn't worth the trouble. It was always funnier the second time. It was extremely funny by the fourteenth.

Reid ate with the careful manner he used at pack gatherings, the manner that meant he was present and engaged, yet slightly elsewhere, the survivor's habit of never being fully off-watch. Harper had noticed this at some point and stopped maneuvering around it, which made Reid more relaxed at pack dinners than Jace had seen him in years.

After dinner, Nora caught him by the door.

"Stop parking across the street," she said, without preamble.

He opened his mouth.

"I drive past the store on my way in from the east road," she said. "I see your truck. Not every day. Enough." She said it plainly, the observation accurate and offered without edge. "You're not avoidant anymore. So stop looking it."

He looked at her. She was right, and he knew she was right, and there was no point in arguing with Nora about matters she was right about. "I went in on Saturday," he said.

"I know." She picked up her coat from the hook by the door. "She told Earl you salted the steps."

He hadn't known that.

"She noticed that you were there," Nora said. "That's the point." She put on the coat. "Go home, Jace. Sleep. Do the north boundary check with Reid tomorrow. And then stop managing this situation and be in it."

She went out.

He stood in the hallway, thinking about what she had said. Stop managing this situation and just be in it. It was easier said than done. He had been managing situations since he was twenty-two, when Cole became Alpha and the responsibility of being Beta settled on him. Managing situations was one of the skills he was good at, possibly too good at.

She said to be in it, his wolf growled. *Not manage it.*

He knew. He knew the difference. He was working on the difference.

He sat with his coffee after everyone had gone and the kitchen was quiet, and let himself think about what he had not been thinking about through the whole dinner, Amanda.

Not her face. Not the word she had used. He had let himself stop replaying those moments about three years ago, after he had understood that the replay wasn't protective but corrosive, that he wasn't preventing it from happening again by reliving it but training himself to expect it everywhere.

What he thought about now was what he had told her, not how she had received it. How he had told her.

Trail outside Glacier, three miles in. The moment had felt right because she had been laughing and the light had been good, and he had thought, *now, while she's happy.* As though the happiness were a buffer that would absorb the impact.

It hadn't been a buffer.

He hadn't told her badly because he had been reckless. He had told her badly because he hadn't understood that asking someone to be your mate requires building the context before you state the fact. You don't hand someone a word like mate in the middle of a forest, what it means, what it would ask of her life, what she would be giving up and what she would be taking on, and expect it to land anywhere but in terror. You build toward it. You let them see the person first. You let them accumulate enough of who you actually are so that when the question comes, it has somewhere to live. He hadn't done that with Amanda. He was going to do it right with Lily.

He was already doing it, he thought.

The inventory reorganization she'd done, the careful questions she'd been asking Earl and Dottie were all part of a pattern she was waiting for to emerge. She was building toward the truth on her own. He had to stay close enough to be the one who handed it to her when she was ready, rather than letting the town do it for him or having her arrive at it on her own with no context and no him.

She already knows the situation is different, his wolf said.

He knew. That was the point.

He drove home through a town that was quiet at nine on a Friday, the streetlights doing their work against the dark, the mountains invisible but present as they were always present, making themselves known through the cold they sent down from the snowline. The tin of coffee from Saturday was on his kitchen counter. He hadn't made it yet. He hadn't wanted to use it up.

He turned on the light in the cabin, stood in the kitchen, and thought about Lily Thornton saying okay, the way she'd said it, which wasn't a woman who was accepting an indefinite delay but a woman who was extending him patience that had a beginning and would at some point have an end, and that he would be a fool not to use it well.

He was going to do this right.

He was going to be in it.

He made the coffee.

He had been putting off making it since Saturday, keeping it on the counter where he could see it, which was a habit he recognized as slightly absurd and had done anyway. A tin of coffee he had bought to have a reason to stay at the counter a few minutes longer. He had bought it with correct change, which was progress from the first visit, and the wrong batteries and the overpayment of thirteen dollars and fifty-eight cents.

The coffee was good. Better than his usual. He stood in the cabin kitchen he had built, drank it, looked out the window at the dark tree line, and thought about being in it.

He was in it.

He didn't entirely know how to be in it as Nora meant it, which was without the management layer, without the calculation, without the careful pacing of information disclosure he had been running. He was going to have to learn. He was thirty-one years old, and he had spent years behind a wall he had built for good reasons, and he wasn't going to dissolve that wall in a week. But he could start with the next step. He could go to the store on a legitimate errand and stay for the conversation that would happen. He could answer her questions honestly when she asked them, which she was going to do, because she was Lily Thornton and she had been filing information about him since the first day she turned and found him there.

He rinsed the mug, put it on the drying rack, turned off the kitchen light, and went to bed.

His wolf was quiet. It had been quiet this way all evening, the settled patience of a creature that had waited a long time and could see that the waiting was ending. Not done. But ending.

He turned off the light and went to bed.

SEVEN

FORCED PROXIMITY

Earl announced on Saturday morning that the shelving units in the back needed to be moved.

This was news to Lily, who had been in the back room several times a week and hadn't noticed any urgency with the shelving units. She said as much. Earl said they had needed to be moved since September, which was before she arrived, making the timing of this announcement feel less coincidental than it might otherwise appear.

"And Jace Mercer is coming to help," she said.

"He offered," Earl said.

"When?"

"Yesterday." Earl didn't elaborate. He moved to the counter with the ease of a man who had said everything he intended to say and wouldn't be adding to it.

Lily looked at him. "You're transparent, you know."

"I'm your grandfather," he said. "Transparency is a privilege."

She went to make coffee.

Jace arrived at nine-thirty with a truck bed full of miscellaneous gear, a man who had prepared himself for the work ahead and was ready to proceed. Lily opened the door. They looked at each other for the half-second that had become their particular rhythm, the one in which both of them processed what was happening and reached a shared, unspoken understanding, and then she stepped back and he came in.

"Earl's in the back," she said.

"Good." His gaze swept the front of the store, the shelves she had reorganized in her first week. "The frequency layout works."

"It needed to."

"I know. Earl's system was held together with—" He stopped. "He'd been meaning to fix it for a while."

She appreciated the edit.

Earl appeared from the back with visible relief. He explained what needed to happen with the shelving units, a project that required more than one person. The first of the larger units needed to move six inches to the left to accommodate a new electrical outlet he had been planning to add since the previous spring. The second one was going against the far wall.

He marked the floor first, two pencil lines showing where each unit should land, then straightened. "I'll be behind the counter," he said. "It's Saturday."

Lily looked at him. He went behind the counter. She

picked up one end of the nearest shelving unit and looked at Jace.

"Six inches," she said.

"Six inches," he confirmed.

They moved shelving units.

The work took two hours.

It wasn't complicated work, but it required coordination. Coordination required communication, which turned out to be different from what either of them had expected. They fell into it without discussion. She read the space, he read the physics, and neither wasted movement. She knew how to work with whoever was next to her without explaining herself. He had spent years on a rescue team where the same was true.

It was the most comfortable she had been around him.

She noticed this while they were carrying the first unit, which was heavier than the first and required more attention to balance. His hands were near hers on the frame. The coordination of moving a heavy unit in a small space together, the mutual adjustment of weight and angle, and how you had to read the other person's next move, not just your own.

"Left a bit," she said.

"Yep."

"Stop."

"Got it."

He moved his half of the unit to the new marks Earl

had made on the floor. She moved hers. They stepped back to look at the result.

"Good," she said.

"Yeah."

He was better at the work than she had expected, a fact she immediately recognized as her having expected the wrong outcome. He was the Beta of a wilderness rescue team. He had built his cabin himself. He was good at reading space and weight and determining where objects needed to go. She noted the correction.

Earl appeared in the doorway. "That's the one," he said. "The second one goes against that wall."

They moved the second one.

THEY FINISHED BEFORE NOON. At some point during the second move, Earl had gone back to the counter and left them to it, which was so characteristic of Earl that Lily had stopped noticing it. The back room was quieter now, and the units in their new positions had opened up a space near the door that had been cramped before.

She was looking at the new layout when Jace said, "Why did you leave?"

She turned. He was leaning against the wall near the new outlet, hands in his pockets. He hadn't entirely planned to ask that. She could see it in how he held himself.

"Bozeman?" she asked.

"The ER."

She considered the question. She had given people the short version since she'd left, needed a change, helping family, took some time. She had given Dottie the real version, which was that she had walked out of a twelve-hour shift one Tuesday and, with the clarity of exhaustion, understood that she had been running on empty for months and hadn't noticed because the work had been too loud to hear it.

She gave him the real version.

Not all of it. But the shape of it. How the work had changed, or she had changed, or both, and how she hadn't understood that until she had been sitting in her apartment for two hours with no idea what she was waiting for, calling Earl, and hearing his *mm* that meant *I was wondering when you'd ask.*

When she finished, he said, "What was the shift?"

She turned. "What?"

"The one you walked out of. What was the case?"

Nobody had ever asked that. The people she had told the story to had focused on the decision, the leaving, the break. He had gone to the moment before the moment.

She told him about the shift. A fourteen-year-old who had come in with chest pain that should have been straightforward but wasn't, the six hours of not-knowing before the answer emerged, and how she had been good throughout it, precise and present. Afterward, when it was resolved and the boy was stable, she had gone to the supply room and stood there for four minutes, unable to explain why she couldn't move.

"Did you go back in?" he asked.

"Yes. I finished the shift."

He nodded. "And then you called Earl."

"Yes, weeks later." She had thought she was fine until she wasn't. "You do that. In that work. You think you're managing and then one day you're not, and you don't know when the gap opened."

She had the sense that he was running a parallel in his mind, one he was deciding whether to speak.

"I know how that works," he said. Not a story. Just the acknowledgment.

She studied him. He held her gaze with the quality he had when he spoke from the center of himself, not from the easy surface he showed the world. She had been cataloging the difference. She knew what it looked like now.

"I think you do," she said.

Dottie appeared in the doorway.

Her eyes moved between them with the expression of a woman who had been expecting to find exactly this and was satisfied with the finding. "Some choices," she said, "you never stop wondering about. Best to make them anyway."

She went back to the front of the store.

Jace and Lily stood in the reorganized back room, with the new electrical outlet and the shelving units in their correct positions, both of them quiet after Dottie's line still in the air.

"She's been doing that my whole life," Lily said.

"She's been doing it to me, too." His expression was that of a man who had been handed a truth he recognized. "I think she plans them."

"I think she does too."

He was reaching for a box on the lower shelf when his hand landed on hers.

They had been working their way through the third section of inventory, consolidating the overflow stock that had accumulated in the corner. At the same moment, she had the same idea about the same box, and his hand came down on the back of hers before either of them had noticed the other was moving.

Neither of them pulled away.

He was aware of her hand under his, of the ordinary temperature of a person, not the elevated temperature his body ran.

Ours, his wolf growled.

She caught his eye.

He pulled his hand back. She did the same half a second later, and neither of them said anything. They went back to what they were doing while acknowledging their connection without naming it.

His phone rang.

He answered because he had been avoiding checking it. Cole had been on the boundary with Reid all morning, which was where Jace was supposed to have been. The protocol required being reachable, and he was reachable here. It wasn't Cole. It was Danny, with a question about the equipment roster that could absolutely have waited but hadn't, because Danny's relationship with urgency was idiosyncratic. He excused himself and stepped toward the front door.

Through the frame, he could see Lily, her phone now at her ear, when the tone of a conversation changed. She stepped to the far end of the room. Her voice was too low to hear.

He dealt with Danny's question, ended the call, and waited.

When she came back, her face had the look it got when she had absorbed new information and was deciding what to do with it.

"My father," she said.

"Everything okay?"

"He's been pulling more property records." She said it neutrally, her tone that of a woman reporting data rather than processing it before a witness. "He found a cross-reference between the land trust and a company formed in 1987. Blackpine Wilderness Rescue, LLC."

Jace didn't say anything. He kept his expression easy.

"That's the year you started the rescue operation," she said. It wasn't a question.

"Cole took over. After our father passed." He said it with the straightforwardness that was true, but also not the whole picture. "He needed a purpose."

She watched him steadily. The nurse's assessment. The cataloging. He could feel her running the data against what she already knew.

"My father thinks there's a pattern in your family's relationship to this town," she said. "I've thought that since I was about twelve."

"Most people from Blackpine do."

"Most people from Blackpine also seem to know things that no one is talking about."

"Yes," he said.

He looked up. She was already watching.

"You said you owed me an explanation," she said.

"I do."

"Are you getting closer to being ready?"

He thought about what Nora had said the night before. *Stop managing this situation and just be in it.* He thought about the fourteen-year-old with chest pain, the supply room, and the gap that opened without warning when you had been running empty for too long. He thought about Lily Thornton saying *okay* with the patience of a woman who had waited her whole life for matters to resolve into clarity and had learned that timing mattered.

"Yes," he said. "I'm getting closer."

She nodded once. Clean. She had heard what she needed to hear, and she was updating her file accordingly.

They finished the inventory. She made coffee. He stayed to drink it, which was a choice he had been telling himself he was going to make and was now making, the execution of *being in it* rather than *managing it from a careful distance.* They sat at the small table in the back and talked about nothing particularly significant for forty minutes, BWR calls from the past month, the inventory she had been planning, the huckleberry pie at Marge's that she hadn't yet had. He told her it was the best thing in Blackpine. She looked at him like she was deciding whether to believe this.

"The best part," she said.

"You'll see."

Her expression held the beginning of a smile. He went home at two in the afternoon with the quiet that came from having spent time with her.

She's worth it, his wolf observed.

He didn't argue.

~

AFTER HE LEFT, she washed the mugs.

This was, she was aware, a small task after a day that had been larger than its surface suggested. She had moved shelving units and told him the real version of the story she had been giving people the short version of since she'd left Bozeman. He had asked the question nobody had asked, and Dottie had appeared in the doorway with her precise timing and her line about choices. They had sat at the small table in the back and talked for forty minutes about nothing significant, as people do when what they are actually doing is learning the texture of each other.

She put the mugs away.

Her father's call had added another item to the list in her head, the company formation, the cross-reference to the land trust, the year BWR was founded, the year after the elder Mercer had died. Jace had said Cole had taken over at twenty-two. He had needed a purpose. She stored the pieces.

She was building toward an answer. She could feel the

shape of it getting clearer without having the whole picture yet, as a diagnosis clarified before you had all the data. You knew the direction before you knew the name.

Jace had said *yes*. He was getting closer to being ready to explain.

She understood she was going to let him do it on his schedule. Not because she lacked the capacity to push; she had sat with incommunicative patients in the ER for years and knew how to ask the right questions in the right order to get the information she needed. She was choosing not to push because she had understood, somewhere between the second shelving unit and the coffee, that what was happening here wasn't a diagnostic problem. It was a relationship, one that required a different kind of patience.

She didn't know when she had started thinking of it as a process that required patience rather than a delay she was waiting to end.

She wiped down the table, put the cloth away, and went to the window. The afternoon had taken on the pale gold of late October at altitude, with long, sharp shadows and a light that said the day had been good, even if it didn't explain why. The mountains were out, clear and white and completely indifferent to her current situation.

Some choices, Dottie had said, *you never stop wondering about. Best to make them anyway.*

She had thought, the first time she heard it, that it was about the Mercers, about Dottie's own life, or about the feel of Blackpine that kept people even when they tried to leave.

She understood now that it was about a truth more particular than any of that.

She turned out the light in the back room and went to check on the store.

EIGHT

THE TRAP

The northern boundary ran eleven miles between the pack's territory and the national forest border, and Jace had run it so many times over the years that his wolf knew every turn as his human body knew the cabin's layout, the knowledge in his muscles and his nose rather than in his mind, without having to think.

He ran it on Wednesday morning because the trail cameras had been running clean since Reid and Cole replaced the offline unit the previous weekend, because Cole had asked for a full boundary read before the end of the week, and because running was one of the activities that helped him think. Not think clearly, exactly. Think at the right pace, which was different. His wolf set the speed. At that pace, his mind could do what it needed to do, usually less than it tried to do at human pace.

What it was doing this morning was the same work it had been doing since Saturday, the problem of how to tell Lily.

Not whether. He was past whether. He had been past whether since the moment he sat across from her in the back of the store, watched her hold a cup of coffee, and listened to him say things he hadn't said out loud to another person in six years, and found that the wall he had been maintaining was costing him more than he had thought. He had driven home from the store like a man who had looked at a truth he had been avoiding for weeks and found it wasn't what he had been afraid of.

He was going to tell her. The question was when and how. He had promised himself he would do it right. Doing it right meant building toward it, not arriving with no context, not handing her a word that would land in a vacuum. He had learned the hard way what a vacuum did to a word like that.

This week, his wolf said.

He was aware of the pressure. Dottie was improving. The whole town knew it. The reason Lily had for being here was shortening on one end while lengthening on the other in ways that had nothing to do with Dottie, and he wasn't going to wait until the Dottie end had shortened enough to force the question. He was going to tell her before then. He had a plan.

He was running the corridor between the second and third trail markers, moving fast through pine and frozen ground cover, when the scent hit him.

He stopped.

Steel. Not the casual iron smell of machinery or old equipment. This was recent, spring-loaded metal, the sharp, cold scent of a mechanism wound tight. He had smelled it twice in this corridor over the past month. Both times in slightly different locations, both times in the stretch of the boundary that ran closest to the northern access road.

He moved off the trail, slower now, nose working. The scent track led him forty feet east of the trail marker, behind a boulder shelf where the snow lay undisturbed except for the prints of an animal that had come through recently and had not gone back the same way.

The wolf was gray, a natural wolf, young adult in size. It had gone still in the frozen way of an animal that has exhausted its struggle and was waiting. The leg-hold trap had caught it above the left foreleg. The mechanism was a double-coil spring, commercial grade, not equipment a weekend hunter would bring in from the hardware store. This was equipment ordered with a purpose.

He shifted back to human form. The cold was immediate, and he ignored it. He had spent enough time on patrol in wolf form to stop noticing the temperature shift, or to notice it and file it as information rather than discomfort. He crouched to the animal's level and held still.

The wolf watched him. Its breath was fast. One ear was flattened; the other tracked him.

"I know," he said, quietly. Not talking to it as people talk to pets. Talking as he talks to the pack, to creatures that understand presence rather than words, that need to know from his stillness that he isn't a threat.

He worked the trap one-handed, the release mechanism at the base of the spring plate. The wolf made a sound, not a yelp but an exhale of tension held too long, and the leg came free.

He sat back. The wolf stayed on the ground, breathing. He stayed where he was, letting it run its own timeline. The cache was in the hollow of the boulder shelf at his back. He reached into it without looking, dressed by feel in the quiet while the wolf decided what it was going to do.

After a minute, it stood. Tested the leg. Took a step, then another. The limp was pronounced, but the leg held. It looked at him with the look of a wild animal that had decided he wasn't what it feared and was adjusting its categories accordingly. Then it turned and moved into the tree line, not running, choosing its pace carefully.

He watched it go. He held the trap in his hands.

Second one this month, his wolf said.

He knew. Same corridor. Same professional-grade. The previous one had been on the trail itself; this one was forty feet off, set along a natural movement route behind cover. Someone had observed the territory, understood the patterns, and set up the equipment accordingly. This wasn't a hunter who had wandered onto pack land unaware. This was someone who had come back.

He started back toward the access road where he had left the truck, turning the information over in his mind as he ran.

SHE HAD BEEN MEANING to go since Nora mentioned it in her third week. Come by BWR sometime. Harper would like to see you. She hadn't gone because she had been working, busy, and, if she was honest with herself, uncertain whether what she would find there would add to the list she was building or complicate it.

She decided Wednesday afternoon to stop being uncertain.

Earl was in the back doing inventory, and when she said she was going to drive out to BWR, he said *"mm,"* as he had when he had been expecting this for a while and was satisfied she had arrived at it.

The access road to BWR ran along the edge of national forest land, a road that had been there long enough to have its own character, with the lean of the pines on either side, how it dipped at the creek crossing and rose again into the open stretch where the mountains were visible to the north. She had driven this road a handful of times over the years, coming back for holidays, and it had always been the same road, unchanged, as certain things in Blackpine were.

She slowed at the creek crossing and saw the truck.

She recognized it. Jace's truck, the BWR-marked one, pulled off the road's right shoulder into a natural cutout between two pines. Engine off. The truck looked like it had been there a while.

She slowed further. There was no reason to stop. Except that she stopped.

She killed her engine and got out.

The sound of the forest in late October was its own kind of quiet, no insects, the birds reduced to winter ones, a stillness that felt active rather than empty. She moved toward the tree line without making a conscious decision. Her nurse's instincts had always been better than her conscious mind at responding to situations that weren't clearly wrong but weren't the default.

She heard him before she saw him. Not footsteps. Breath. And then a stillness that came from a person choosing stillness rather than finding it.

She stopped at the edge of the boulder shelf.

He was crouched on the ground, about ten feet from the road. In front of him stood a gray wolf, young, one foreleg held close to its body, watching him with the flattened-ear focus of an animal not yet ready to trust the person in front of it. Jace held a metal object in his right hand that she couldn't see from this angle. His held hand out, palm down. Not reaching. Offering.

The wolf moved. One step. Another. The limp was clear, but the leg held.

Jace sat back. Watched. Didn't move.

She knew the difference between a person who was controlling their stillness because they were afraid and one whose stillness came from somewhere deeper, a presence practiced and real. Jace Mercer didn't look like a man afraid of the wolf in front of him. He seemed like a man in conversation with it in a language that didn't require words.

The wolf turned and moved into the trees. He watched it go.

She must have made some sound, the shift of gravel under her boot or the change in the air, because he turned.

His eyes found hers. His expression was completely

unguarded, as if he were caught in a private act, and then his face settled into a more familiar look. But not before she had seen it. Whatever had been in his face when the wolf walked away, a rawness undone and without a category, she had seen it.

"Lily." He got to his feet. "I didn't know you'd be on this road."

"I was going to see Harper." Her look went to where the wolf had disappeared. "Is it all right?"

He looked at the object in his hand. She could see it now, a trap. Double-coil spring, leg-hold, the jaws slightly open. She recognized the mechanism from her third-year wilderness medicine rotation. The instructor had covered trap injuries and hadn't been gentle about it.

"Front leg," he said. "It'll hold. Young animal, otherwise healthy."

"The trap is commercial grade." Not a question. A notation.

He met her eyes. "Yes."

"Someone set it."

"Someone who knows this territory." He said it the same way he did when he gave her the full information without the full explanation. She had cataloged this quality in him over the past month. He didn't lie to her. He withheld. There was a difference, and she had noted it.

She studied him. His hair had pine needles in it. His jacket was open, and the cold wasn't reaching him as it should have, but she wasn't cataloging that yet; she was filing it.

"The trap was set for the wolf?" she asked.

"I think so. This is the second one this month in the same corridor." He turned it over in his hands. "We're going to need to report it. The natural wolf population in this territory gets informal protection from the pack, from BWR." The correction was smooth enough that she almost didn't notice it. Almost. "Poaching activity up here has been quiet for a few years. This is new."

Her look moved to his hands. To the trap. To the place where the wolf had gone.

"You knew how to work it," she said.

"I've had to do this before."

"More than once."

"More than once."

She filed it. *He handles wild animals like he is one of them.* Not a metaphor. A fact she was keeping.

"I'm sorry you saw it caught," he said. "It's not—" He stopped. "It shouldn't have been caught."

She understood what he meant. The alternative was worse. She had made her peace with the difference between what should have happened and what to do about what actually happened a long time ago, in the third hour of a shift, when the should-haves were already out the window and only the available options remained. You worked with what you had.

"Will you tell Cole?" she asked.

"Tonight." He pocketed the trap. Looked at her. "You going to see Harper?"

"Yes."

"She'll want to hear about this." He said it with an

expression that wasn't quite a smile. "She always wants to hear about anything that happened on the territory."

Lily looked at the tree line where the wolf had gone and thought about how it had walked away. Careful, choosing its pace. It had known where it was going.

She got in the truck. She had been going to see Harper. She went home instead.

He reported to Cole that evening.

Cole heard him out, his expression the same as when information confirmed a suspicion he had been expecting and didn't like. He turned the trap over on the table between them, as Jace had turned it over in the field, reading it.

"Same stretch," Cole said.

"East side, forty feet off the trail marker. Placed at the movement route behind the boulder shelf." Jace sat back. "It's not random placement. Someone read the territory."

Cole was quiet. Reid, who had come in from the equipment room when he heard Jace's truck, leaned against the doorframe with his coffee, wearing the look he got when he was running information in parallel. He said, "The previous one was on the trail itself."

"Slightly east of center."

"Moving the placement east," Reid said, as if he were reading a map. "Two data points aren't a pattern. Three is."

"Then we need to find the third before it catches

another wolf." Cole set the trap down. His attention shifted to Jace. "Lily was on the access road."

It wasn't a question. The pack information network ran at Blackpine's speed, which was faster than most people expected.

"She was going to see Harper," Jace said. "She saw me with the natural wolf. Not—" He held his expression. "Not the earlier part. The freeing."

Cole studied him. "How did she take it?"

"She took it as she takes everything." He thought about her face as the wolf walked away, how she had watched it go, as if adding a fact to a list she was keeping, a detail that fit into a space she had already made for it. "She asked the right questions."

Cole nodded. He didn't say anything about the Saturday dinner Jace had told him he was planning. He didn't need to.

"Reid," Cole said. "I want a sweep of the full northern corridor by Friday. Map the placement logic."

Reid nodded. He would do it in wolf form, in the dark, and by Thursday morning he would have a map on the table that would tell them whether the trap placement was systematic or opportunistic. If it was systematic, someone was returning. If they were returning, they hadn't found what they were looking for yet.

Jace drove home with that thought and the image of the wolf moving into the trees, the careful pace of it, the held leg, choosing.

She saw, his wolf rumbled.

He had watched Lily's face as the wolf walked away.

The filing excellence of it, the nurse's precision. But beneath that, a deeper recognition, the expression of someone seeing a truth that had been in their peripheral vision, unnamed. He had seen that expression before. He had been waiting for it, without knowing he was waiting for it, for weeks.

He pulled into his driveway and sat with the engine ticking down. The trap sat on the passenger seat. Reid had looked at it at the table, but looking wasn't the same as having it at the workbench. He would leave it with him in the morning. Reid would read the spring mechanism as he read everything, with the patience of a man who understood that the answer you were looking for was usually in what you could observe rather than in what you could deduce.

She saw the wolf walk away, his wolf said.

He knew. The wolf had limped toward the trees, choosing its pace, and Lily Thornton had watched it with the expression of a woman who was seeing a truth she hadn't had a name for and was beginning to understand that it had a name. He didn't know what the name was on her side. On his side, the name was mate.

Soon.

NINE

THE LONG WAY

He came in on Thursday afternoon.

Not for batteries. Not for coffee, though he ordered one from the burner behind the counter and paid with the correct change. He sat at the counter like a man who had decided to do a task and was doing it without needing permission. She had noted this about him, he didn't need an excuse to be where he had chosen to be. He came in,and the answer he gave when she asked what he needed was always technically true and never quite the real answer.

"The wolf," she said. She had gone back to the inventory she'd been working through before he arrived. "How is it?"

"It'll be fine." He turned his coffee cup. "Front leg traps heal clean if the joint's not compromised. It wasn't."

"You checked."

"I know the territory it went into." He didn't explain further.

She wrote a number on the inventory sheet and moved to the next line. The store was quiet at this hour, with Earl in the back working through the month-end accounts and the cast-iron stove doing its work in the corner. The light through the front window had turned the flat gray of late October afternoons, a light that made the inside of the store feel more like itself, cozy and enclosed.

"Did you grow up running that territory?" she asked.

"Most of it. The northern boundary from the time I could run it reliably." He paused. "Cole started me at nine. Said the boundary was a lesson you learned with your feet, not off a map."

She thought about the boy he would have been at nine, running eleven miles of territory with the older brother who would become Alpha. She had seen Cole at nine, or around then, during the summers she came back. She hadn't paid enough attention to Cole at nine to learn much about him. She had paid more attention to Jace, even then, without fully understanding why.

"You said your father built the cabin," she said.

"The first one. What's standing now I rebuilt years ago." He drank the coffee. "After some events, I needed to do work with my hands."

She noted the framing. *After some events.* She had been in emergency medicine long enough to recognize that phrasing, how someone talked around a time that didn't have a clean name. She had used it herself, in the months before she called Earl. *Life happened. I needed a change.*

She didn't push. She went back to her inventory and let him sit there with his coffee.

"You grew up coming back for summers," he said after a while.

"Every year until I was eighteen."

"And the rest of the year you were in Bozeman."

"With my mother." She wrote down a count without looking up. "She moved there when I was eleven. My parents split. It was a split that didn't leave much room for halfway. I spent the school year in Bozeman and the summers here."

"Which did you like better?"

She met his eyes. He was watching her with the quality he had when he was asking a question he actually wanted the answer to, not the conversational kind.

"Here," she said. "I always liked it better here. Bozeman was where I grew up. This was where I was from."

He nodded. Like he had known that.

"There's a trail," he said. "Past the western property line, where our land meets the national forest. It opens up above the tree line into a clearing that looks out over the full northern range. My father used to bring us there on clear days." He turned the cup again. "You should come sometime."

She waited.

"When I can take you properly."

She noted it. The same construction as *do it right* and *not until you know* and *soon*.

"I'd like that," she said, and went back to the inventory.

She was aware of him, as she had been for five weeks,

the peripheral awareness of a person whose presence you have decided to stop cataloging, only to keep cataloging anyway. He had his coffee and the ease of a man who didn't feel the need to fill silence.

"You were around a lot," she said. "When we were kids. When I came back for the summer."

"You were hard to miss," he stated, looking at the inventory sheet.

"I noticed you more than I probably let on." Her eyes dropped to the inventory sheet. "That's an honest statement, not a flattering one."

"I know the difference." He was quiet a moment. "You were always going to leave again. That was the part I understood."

Her eyes lifted. He wasn't watching her with anything she could easily categorize. He had the quality he took on when he was speaking a truth he meant from the center of himself rather than from the easy surface. She had learned to recognize it. She was recognizing it now.

"I left a lot behind in Blackpine," she said.

He didn't answer. He drank his coffee.

He stayed until Earl came out from the back, and then they talked for ten minutes about the delivery schedule, the road conditions before the first hard snow, and whether the hardware store would have storm window sealer in stock before November, a recurring concern. She listened without appearing to listen. This was another skill she had learned in the ER, how people were with each other when they'd known each other a long time. Jace and Earl moved through the conversation with the ease of two people who didn't need to establish anything, who could start in the middle of things because there was no beginning that wasn't already understood.

He left at quarter past four. She watched the door close.

~

Friday, Earl had a standing supply run to BWR.

She had known he did this, peripherally, as you know facts you have stored without examining them. Earl kept the general store's supply relationship with BWR as one of the long-standing business arrangements in his ledger, one that had been there longer than she could remember and that he managed with discretion. What BWR needed wasn't always what was itemized on a standard invoice. She hadn't asked for details because she had been waiting for the right time.

Friday after closing, Earl looked up from the register. "Coming with me this week?"

She went to get her coat.

The drive out to BWR took twenty minutes on the mountain road, the same road she had taken on Wednesday. She watched the light go out of the sky in the west as they climbed. Earl drove as he did most things, with complete attention and no wasted movement, and he didn't explain where they were going or what the arrangement was. She didn't ask. She had stopped needing him to explain things to her in sequence. He would tell her what she needed to know when she needed to know it, and she had come to trust this about him, the same trust she had in the way certain patients knew when to speak and when to hold their information.

The HQ came into view through the pines, a cluster of buildings, the main structure large and low, with lights in the windows, and several vehicles in the dirt lot, including the one she recognized as Jace's. The space had the feel of a place that had been used hard for a long time. Not worn out. Worn in. There was a difference.

Earl pulled up near the equipment building. A man she recognized as Reid Webb came out to meet them, nodded to Earl, lifted two crates from the truck bed efficiently. He studied her with the steady look of a man assessing a situation and reaching a conclusion. "Coming in?" he asked.

She turned to Earl.

"Nora's expecting the delivery," Earl said. "Might as well say hello."

She followed Reid inside.

The main room was heated and larger than it looked from outside, with the comfort of a space heated for the people who used it rather than for appearances. A long table ran nearly the length of the room. The kitchen opened off the far end, and from it came the smell of stew that had been cooking for a while. Nora Callahan came out of it holding a wooden spoon, saw Lily, and said, flat and satisfied, "Good. You can help with the rolls."

Lily took off her coat.

She hadn't been in this space before. She had known BWR existed, as everyone in Blackpine did, as a presence in the town's life and a significant feature of the Mercer family's story, but she hadn't been inside it. What she found wasn't what she had expected, even though she hadn't known she had expected anything; she had expected a facility organized for function, and what she found was a home. A large home, one that had been lived in by more than one person for a long time, with the traces of ongoing life layered over each other, as they were in places where people actually belonged to each other.

Harper Stone-Mercer sat at the end of the table with a laptop open, and she looked up when Lily came in. Her expression was open in that way that was distinctly Harper's, the directness of a woman who said what she meant and was glad to see you. "Lily. Finally." She said it the way you say it to someone who has been expected for a while.

The rest of the evening came in pieces, as evenings did when you were somewhere new and paying attention. Cole Mercer moving between the equipment room and the kitchen with the economy of a man on whose shoulders a great deal rested, who had learned to carry it without visible effort. Danny, whom she placed as the youngest person in the room within the first thirty seconds, and who was also clearly competent enough that the youngest-person part had stopped being the defining characteristic. Old Tom in the chair nearest the fire, telling a story she arrived in the middle of about a bear and a set of circumstances that somehow ended with the bear leaving in apparent satisfaction. Reid at the edge of things, present and slightly elsewhere, with the watchfulness of a man who had never fully learned to be off-watch.

Harper caught her in the hallway near the kitchen, after the meal and before people had started to leave.

"He's a good man," Harper said, without preamble. She had, Lily was learning, a journalist's instinct for the sentence that saved time. "He's been trying to figure out how to do this right for a while."

Lily looked at her. "How long is a while?"

Harper looked back at her. She didn't answer. But the look itself was the answer, longer than you know, and the knowing of it is his to hand you.

Lily tucked it away.

SHE FOUND HIM OUTSIDE, her coat over her arm.

He was leaning against the near side of the truck, looking at the tree line, his hands in his jacket pockets. He turned when he heard her steps on the gravel.

"Good night?" he asked.

"Yes." She pulled on her coat. The air had the bite of the temperature dropping, the sky clear and dark above the pines. "I like them."

"They like you." He said it like a fact he was reporting. "Nora's been saying she wanted to meet you since your first week."

"She said she wanted help with rolls."

"That's Nora's version of the same thing."

She buttoned her coat. He remained there, not quite between her and the door. The night was cold. In the low light from the HQ windows, his eyes had that look she had been noticing for weeks, the amber hue beneath the ordinary brown. She had stopped pretending she didn't notice.

Earl had gone back inside; she could hear voices through the lit windows of the main building.

She held his gaze.

"Not yet," he said.

She breathed out. "You keep saying that."

"I know."

"Soon, you said."

He held her attention. "I know. Soon."

She understood what he meant, even without the context. He was doing what he had promised to do, which was to do it right, and he was close to the right time, and she had enough patience left for it.

She didn't have unlimited patience. She knew the difference between waiting because you didn't know what came next and waiting because you knew exactly what came next and were allowing someone the time to arrive at the same conclusion.

"All right," she said, and got in the truck.

She heard him behind her, his footsteps retreating toward the HQ, and she watched the building in the side mirror as Earl came out, got in, started the engine, and drove them back down the mountain road in the dark, the trees pressing in on either side, the sky clear above. She was in the second kind of wait. It had a different nature. It had a different end.

She hadn't been thinking about Bozeman, she realized. Not the way she had expected to, as a fixed point waiting for her return. The apartment, the hospital, the rhythm of a life she understood. When she first arrived she had held it that way, the permanent life in another place. She wasn't holding it that way now.

She was thinking about Harper's look. Longer than you know. That look, which wasn't pity, wasn't a warning, and wasn't even particularly personal, was the look of a woman who knew the full story and was offering a piece of it.

She was thinking about how he had said *I left a lot behind in Blackpine* and he hadn't argued.

She turned that over. She wasn't a person who made meaning out of events carelessly. She worked with evidence. She built pictures from what was observable, and she didn't name the picture until she had enough of it. She was beginning to have enough of it.

Earl drove. The road ran down the mountain. The pines on both sides moved past in the dark, steady and familiar, the same road she had driven her whole childhood, and it had the same feel it always had; a road that knew where it was going.

TEN

COUNTDOWN

Frank called at noon on Friday, as he always did, at the exact midpoint of her day, as though he had built his schedule around hers and was too precise a man to deviate from it. She had answered his calls in the same order for twenty-odd years, how are you, how is Dottie, how is the work. The answers were routine. What changed lately was what came after the routine.

"I went back to the 1987 filing," he said.

She had been expecting this. Her father was a county assessor who had spent nineteen years in the discipline of public records, and when he found an anomaly he didn't leave it. He returned. He examined the same document from different angles until the angle that revealed the pattern presented itself.

"The company formation," she said.

"The signatories." Satisfaction in his voice. His research had finally turned up the piece it needed. "The 1987 filing for Blackpine Wilderness Rescue, LLC. It lists three names. Cole Mercer, as primary. The other two are listed as silent partners. Standard enough. But one of them is tied to the same land trust that predates the county, not as a trustee but as an original grantor."

Lily put down the pen she had been using on the inventory sheet. "Meaning the trust was funded by someone who later became a silent partner in BWR."

"Meaning the legal framework goes back further than 1987, and the 1987 filing wasn't the beginning of it. It was the formalization of an arrangement that already existed." He paused. "I went further back. There's a 1942 county land survey for that parcel. A government document from the Bureau of Land Management. The notation for the parcel's ownership status reads, held in perpetual family stewardship per prior arrangement. That language doesn't appear anywhere else in the county's land records. I've checked."

"A prior arrangement," she said.

"Prior to 1942, which means prior to anything the county has formal records for in that territory." His voice was even, the voice he used when he was telling her facts he had verified and was certain of. "Someone set a legal framework around that land designed to persist. Not to be bought, sold, or disputed. Just to continue."

"You're not saying anything," Lily said.

"I'm saying what I found." He said it as he always said it when he was minimizing how much effort the work had cost him. "I'm not worried about the records. The records don't tell me anything criminal. They tell me the arrangement is old. What I'm worried about is you being there without understanding what you're in the middle of."

"What do you think I'm in the middle of?"

Silence. "I don't know. That's the part I don't like."

"Dad," she said. "I know what I'm in the middle of."

"That's not the same as knowing."

"No," she said. "But it's where I am."

He was quiet. She could hear him breathing.

"Call me when you know more," he said.

"I will."

After she hung up, she sat with the phone in her hand and looked out the front window at the street. The mountains were visible above the roofline across the road, white and sharp, the sky behind them the hard, clear blue that came with cold fronts.

She had been building a picture for five weeks. She had started it on the first day, with the look on Jace Mercer's face when he walked through the door and encountered someone he hadn't expected. She had added to it incrementally, how the town held certain silences, the information Mrs. Patterson had offered on her first day back, and the ease with which the inner circle moved through the world as though they were larger within their own lives than other people. The land trust. The 1987 filing. How Cole Mercer had taken over the rescue operation at twenty-two because he had needed a purpose. How Jace had said I was strange. I know I was strange, someone who understood that the strangeness required an explanation but couldn't yet give it.

She wasn't at inference yet. The picture wasn't complete. She was still adding to it.

The name was coming.

She put the phone down and went back to the inventory.

The store was quiet. Earl was somewhere in the back. The stove ticked. Outside, the November sky was moving in from the north, the blue hardening at the edges into a gray that would arrive before dark. The mountains were still visible. She watched them for a while, the white of the snowline, the light on the upper slopes in the middle of the day, the color she hadn't seen anywhere else.

She had told her father she was in the middle of figuring it out. That was true. She had also told him she knew what she was in the middle of. That was less true. She knew the shape. She knew the direction. She was waiting for the name.

THE PACK MEETING was on Monday evening, after dinner, at Cole's cabin.

Cole sat at the table with the directness he reserved for matters that needed to be said directly, which was most matters. He had a map of the northern corridor on the table, along with Reid's work from the Thursday sweep, the trap placement logic marked with Reid's careful notation, methodical, pattern-mapped. Three traps in the same corridor over six weeks, moving east and north with each placement. Not random.

"Someone's learning the territory," Reid said, looking at his own map. "The first was on a main trail. The second was off-trail along a natural movement route. The third was at the exact point where any large animal moving east from the second location would naturally pass." Reid's voice was the same as when he reported weather conditions. A fact and its implications, no performance attached. "This is observation plus iteration. They're watching how the territory responds and adjusting."

Cole turned the map. "Any evidence of active surveillance? Visual?"

"Not yet. The placements are spaced far enough apart that they could be doing the observation passes days apart, not concurrently. I'd want another week before I called it a pattern with a person behind it." He looked up. "But it walks like a person."

Cole nodded. He let that sit.

Then his attention shifted to Jace.

"How long?" he said.

Jace had known the question was coming. Cole didn't ask questions he wasn't ready to have answered, and the question of *how long* had been approaching the surface of their conversations for two weeks. He had been the one keeping it below the surface with the deliberate pressure of a man managing a timeline. Cole's patience wasn't unlimited. He had known it wasn't.

"This week," Jace said.

Cole studied him. "You've said this week before."

"Saturday." He said it flat, as he said things when they were decided. "Dinner at the cabin. I'll tell her Saturday."

Nora, at the far end of the table, didn't look up from the logistics notes she was making. "She came to dinner on Friday," she said. "Did you talk to her?"

"Not about that."

"But she was here." She looked up. "She saw the house. She sat at the table. She helped with the bread."

"I know."

"She left a presence." Nora set down her pen. "I don't mean physically. I mean she fits. You can feel it when a person fits." She said it as a fact she had observed for forty-five years. "She fits."

Cole was watching Jace.

"Saturday," Jace said again.

"The Frank Thornton situation," Cole said. "Reid, where are we?"

Reid had a folder. He set it on the table. "Property records research. He traced the 1987 filing and identified the signatories. He's also found the 1942 land survey nota-tion." Reid set the folder on the table. The facts spoke plainly enough without editorial. "He knows the frame-work is old and was designed to persist. He doesn't know what it's for."

Cole turned the folder over. "He'll keep digging."

"He's a county assessor. Digging is what he does." Reid paused. "He hasn't contacted anyone outside Billings with what he's found. It's still private research."

"Lily knows," Cole said.

"He tells her what he finds. She doesn't tell us what she tells him back." His attention turned to Jace. "Do we know what she tells him?"

Jace thought about Lily on the phone in the back of the store, how she kept her voice neutral and her information limited. "She's not alarming him further. She's managing it."

"What does Lily know about what her father has found?" Cole asked.

"She knows about the 1987 filing," Jace said. "She told me directly a couple of weeks ago. She knows Cole started BWR and needed a purpose, and she's been working through what that means." He paused. "She doesn't have the piece about what we are. She has everything around it."

Cole looked at the map. The northern corridor, the trap placements, Reid's annotations. The territory the pack had held for three generations. The territory that held them back.

"She's been here six weeks," Cole said. "In that time, she has reorganized the store, learned the town's information networks, identified the land trust anomaly through her father's research, attended a pack dinner, and made clear she's not thinking about her return date." He said it without judgment. "She's not here anymore as a visitor waiting to leave. She's here as a person who has already made a decision they haven't named yet."

Jace said nothing.

"That's not a criticism," Cole said. "That's why Saturday is the right time. She's ready. The question is whether you are."

Jace looked at the map. The northern boundary ran on it as a clear line, the pack's territory on one side and the national forest on the other. He had run that line his entire life. He knew every creek crossing and boulder shelf and natural movement route. He knew where the traps were. He knew where the wolves moved.

He knew where Lily's truck had been parked on Wednesday. He knew what she had looked like watching the gray wolf choose its pace into the trees.

"I'm ready," he said.

Cole nodded. He closed the folder. He studied the map for a while.

"Saturday," he said. "No later."

Dottie was walking to the window by herself, without the counter to trail her hand along.

It was a small victory. In the first weeks, she had moved through familiar spaces by feel, the counter, the chair back, the stove, each piece of furniture a waypoint. Now she crossed open floor without reaching for anything. The distance between the table and the window wasn't far. She covered it as someone who knew the ground was there and trusted it, and she did it without performance, without the deliberate accounting of each step that had marked the early weeks. She made it to the window and stood there looking out at the street, her right side steady beneath her.

Lily watched her and felt the complicated satisfaction she always felt when a patient improved faster than the timeline, the satisfaction of it, and beneath it, the altered arithmetic. The reason Lily was here was getting shorter.

"I've been thinking," Dottie offered from the window. She was looking out at the street, the mountains beyond the buildings. "When you go back to Bozeman, you should look into the clinic on Kagy Boulevard. They've been looking for a trauma nurse for two years. Janet Kowalski's daughter works there."

Lily didn't say anything.

"It's worth a phone call," Dottie said. "You've been here six weeks. The hospital will have moved on."

Lily looked at the table, at the cup of tea she had made, at the grain of the wood she had sat with her whole life. She knew this table. She knew how the light moved across it in the morning and how it looked at this hour, the late afternoon light from the window. She had eaten thousands of meals at this table.

She hadn't corrected Dottie.

She was aware that she hadn't corrected Dottie. She was aware of it, had opened her mouth to correct Dottie and found the correction wasn't there.

She picked up her tea.

"I'll look into it," she said.

This wasn't a lie. She would look into it. She looked into options. The looking didn't commit her to anything. It was only data. She had told herself this before about other topics she was looking into, and she was aware of the pattern, and she was choosing to let it run a little longer before she named it.

Dottie turned from the window. She moved with the

adapted attention of a woman who knew what her body required of her now and gave it without ceremony. The right side still asked for something. She had stopped arguing with it.

She made her way to her chair and sat.

"You look like you're thinking about someone," Dottie said.

"Just the inventory."

Dottie looked at her with the expression she had worn since Lily was nine years old, the one that knew it was getting the short version of a story and chose not to press. Dottie had always been good at choosing not to press. It was one of the habits Lily had learned from her without realizing she was learning it, the patience of a person who understood that some truths arrived when they were ready and not before.

"The Kagy Boulevard clinic," Dottie said. "It's a good fit for you. Good people. Janet's daughter is happy there."

"I heard you," Lily said.

"I know you did." Dottie picked up her book. "I'm just saying."

Lily drank her tea and didn't say, *I didn't correct you. I noticed I didn't correct you.* She stored it instead, with everything else she had been collecting, in the part of her mind that was holding the open question she didn't yet have the full name for.

She wasn't thinking about what was coming. He would tell her, when he was ready. The one he was working toward. She wasn't thinking about it.

HE CALLED HER TUESDAY EVENING.

He had thought about how to say it and had concluded that the most direct way was the right way, a conclusion he reached every time he thought about Lily Thornton and communication, because she responded better to directness than to preamble.

She answered on the second ring.

"Saturday," he said. "Come to dinner. My cabin."

A pause. Her silence had a weight to it. She was weighing her response.

"All right," she said. "What time?"

"Seven."

"What should I bring?"

"Nothing." He had thought about this too. "I'll have it."

Another pause. Not uncertain. Just how she moved through conversations, careful as someone tracking more than the surface.

"Okay," she said.

He stayed with the phone in his hand after he hung up. His wolf was holding the posture it had been holding since Saturday, the settled patience of a creature that had seen what it was waiting for and understood that patience wasn't the same as passivity. It wasn't waiting for a door to open. It was the state of a person who had a hand on the door and knew what they would say when it opened.

Saturday, his wolf said.

Saturday.

ELEVEN

THE CALL

The pack dinner was quiet that week.

Not the surface of it. The surface was the same, Old Tom's bear story, which Lily had been charmed by the previous Friday and which Tom therefore told again with additions Jace was fairly certain hadn't been in the original version. Danny working through a comms problem at the table, explaining it to Reid with the focused persistence of a man who had decided someone was going to understand this whether they wanted to or not. Reid listening with the particular quality he had when he thought information was relevant to territory security and hadn't yet decided whether to say so.

What was different was Lily. She was in the kitchen with Nora before dinner, not being directed but moving on her own, having learned in one week where things were kept. She had helped plate the food without being asked. She had poured coffee for Old Tom before he'd noticed he wanted any. She was learning the pack's rhythms the way she learned everything, by paying attention until the pattern became automatic.

Cole sat at the end of the table, ate, watched the room, and didn't say anything about Saturday. He didn't need to.

Jace stayed through dinner, through cleanup, and through the end of the evening, when people began to head for coats and keys. As he left, he told Cole, "Northern corridor. I want to do a pass before tomorrow. Reid's map put the third trap at the edge of a new movement zone, and I want to walk it before the frost covers it again."

Cole looked at him. "Alone."

"Fast sweep. Two hours."

Cole considered this for the length of time he usually took when he was deciding whether to trust someone's judgment on a matter on which he had a different read. He said, "Pack bond stays open. If I feel anything off, I'm coming out."

"Fair."

He drove to the trailhead.

The Miller Road access was a four-mile stretch from the main road to the northern boundary, an old fire road that hadn't been formally maintained in twenty years but that BWR kept passable in both directions for exactly this kind of situation. He parked at the trailhead marker, got out, left his jacket and keys on the passenger seat, and ran ahead to the cache point in human form. Standard protocol for a solo night run was to leave your phone closer to the working area, in case something went wrong out there. He left it with the cache jacket, shifted, and went into the dark.

The cold at this hour was different in wolf form, not a factor to be managed but data. The temperature, the wind's direction, the frozen ground cover, and what they told him about the week's weather pattern. He moved fast through the first mile of trail, reorienting to the boundary's feel after a week of running it primarily in human form. His wolf settled into the pace as it always did, with the ease of a creature in its element.

The northern corridor ran eleven miles. Reid's map had the trap placements marked at roughly mile three, mile four, and the projected zone for any further placement at the northeast edge of mile five. That was where he was headed.

He found it at mile four and a half.

Not a trap. The platform for one, a natural depression in the ground, partially concealed by a fallen log, exactly where his wolf's pattern-sense said the next logical placement in the series would be. Someone had been here recently. He could smell it, cold sweat, synthetic fabric, boot rubber, the scent of a person who hadn't been in the woods long enough to stop smelling like the place they'd come from. Two days ago, maybe three.

He was examining the depression when the trap closed on his right hind leg.

He hadn't seen it because it had been placed in the hollow of the log, not on the ground; a second trap, set to catch him at the exact angle of approach he had taken. The spring mechanism was heavier than the others had been. The pain arrived like information, immediate and complete, and his wolf's first response was to pull, the wrong response. He overrode it in the half-second before the pull could do damage. He went still.

He tried to shift.

The pain interrupted it. Not the shift itself, which was voluntary, but the physical capacity to execute it, the transition required a degree of muscular relaxation that the trapped leg refused. He could feel the transformation wanting to begin and the leg holding it back, the two systems fighting each other. He pushed harder and felt the shift stutter partway through, landing him in the unresolvable state in between, one of the worst physical experiences he was capable of having, which he had had exactly twice before in his life and didn't recommend.

He lay with his breathing. He let the pain be what it was without adding to it.

The pack bond was open, as Cole had specified. He could feel Cole through it, distant yet present, not yet alarmed. He hadn't sent anything alarming. He hadn't sent anything at all; the pack bond transmitted emotional state and approximate location, and he had locked his emotional state to the focused, careful demeanor of a man solving a problem, because sending alarm would bring Cole and Reid and Danny and two trucks and a medical kit, and everyone would be there when he was in this state, and he wouldn't be in control of how the evening went.

He pushed forward through the shift. More human was the direction. He needed hands.

It cost him. The partial form resolving forward rather than back wasn't how the shift worked naturally, and his body recognized it as the error it was. But he got there, human enough for hands, for the clothes cache forty feet up the trail, for the jacket inside it and his phone where he'd left it.

He needed the trap freed. He needed one person, not a rescue operation. He called her.

He hadn't planned this. He had planned tomorrow night, dinner at the cabin, the conversation he had built in his head. He had planned it right. This wasn't that.

Two rings. She picked up.

"Lily." His voice came out controlled. The pain was there under it and she was sharp enough to hear it and he didn't try to hide it but he also didn't lead with it. "I need help. I'm at the Miller Road trailhead, north of BWR, about a mile and a half in on the eastern trail. I can't explain what you're going to see when you get here. I need you to come, and I need you to stay."

A pause. Not panic. Assessment.

"Are you in immediate danger?" she asked. Nurse first. He had known this about her.

"No. Injured. Not going anywhere."

"I'll be there in twenty minutes."

She hung up.

He put the phone down, lay back on the cold ground, and looked at the sky through the pine canopy. The stars were visible through the gaps, the hard, clear November sky doing nothing. He had spent a significant portion of his adult life working out the right way to do this, and the right way had always included a warm space, a prepared conversation, and a version of himself fully in control of the framing. He had a cabin. He had made a reservation in his kitchen for tomorrow evening. He had planned sentences.

None of that was going to be how this happened.

Good, his wolf approved.

He held that for a while.

His wolf had never agreed with him on the management strategy. It had been clear about this from the beginning, from the first time he walked into the general store and she turned. He understood with absolute clarity that this was the person, and the wall he had been maintaining was one he had built to survive a wound, and that wound wasn't this. It had wanted to go immediately, and he had held it back with the patience of a man who had learned, at a cost he didn't want to repeat, that how you did a thing mattered as much as the thing.

His wolf wasn't arguing with the principle. It was arguing with the execution.

Maybe it had a point. He had been moving toward Saturday for five weeks, and in that time he had managed to, get caught in a trap he should have seen coming, call the person he had been carefully not overwhelming with urgency at ten o'clock on a Friday night, and set himself up for the most important conversation of the last six years while lying on a forest floor with a trapped and partially shifted hind leg.

She's coming, his wolf said.

She was. He could hear the truck on the access road. He had good hearing even in human form, which was one of the facts he was going to explain tomorrow. Tonight, he was going to have to manage the explaining-tonight version of this, which he hadn't planned and would have to improvise, and he was going to have to trust that she was who he thought she was.

He already knew she was. That was the truth about five weeks of watching Lily Thornton operate in the world. He had accumulated a great deal of evidence.

He lay in the cold and waited, keeping his emotions locked in calm, and thought about how this wasn't how he had planned it and that some part of him, the part that wasn't his wolf or his management instinct but an instinct older than both, had known this was the only way it was ever going to go.

She had been reading when the phone rang.

Not a patient, deliberate book-before-bed read. The unfocused kind of reading she did when her mind was elsewhere, turning pages without retaining them and eventually noticing she had been holding the book for thirty minutes with no idea what she had read. She had been doing this most of the evening. She had told herself she wasn't thinking about Saturday, which was precisely the thought that occupied the part of the mind officially not occupied with anything.

His voice on the phone carried the sound of controlled pain. She had trained herself to hear this in patients, the voice managing pain by keeping it at a distance from the words, the voice of a person who needed help and was being precise about how to ask for it because they had decided precision was more useful than distress.

She didn't ask questions. She took her coat, took the first aid kit from the cabinet behind the counter, went to her vehicle, and drove.

The Miller Road trailhead was twenty-two minutes from the store on roads she had driven recently and knew well enough to take fast in the dark. She parked behind his truck, which was there, meaning he had been here a while. She pulled on her coat, took the kit, and went up the trail with her flashlight.

The trail was clear and the ground was frozen, and she moved fast. She had done wilderness medicine rotations. She knew a night forest in cold November, the sounds that belonged and the sounds that didn't. What she heard as she walked was the wind in the upper branches, the sound of the creek somewhere to the north, her footsteps on the frozen ground. What she didn't hear was anyone in distress. His voice had been controlled. She matched her pace to that.

A mile and a half in, she went off the trail to the right. He was a hundred and fifty yards into the trees. She saw the flashlight reflection on his jacket and adjusted course.

She stopped at six feet, put the light on him, and then stopped entirely.

She was a nurse. She had a clinical vocabulary for what she was looking at, and none of it applied.

He was lying on his side with one leg extended, and the leg wasn't quite right. Not injured-not-right. Structurally not right, in a way her medical training had a word for, except the word her training offered was the wrong one. His leg, she corrected herself, catching the other word before it fully formed, was caught in a leg-hold trap. So was something else. The something else had fur on it and was larger than a leg had any business being.

She took a breath.

Nurse training: assess, act, stabilize. Questions later.

"I'm going to free the trap," she said. Her voice was steady. She made it steady. "Don't move."

He didn't move. He was watching her with eyes that had turned the amber gold she had seen before, the aspect she had been cataloging, and this time there was nothing human about the way they were framed. She looked at the trap, not the eyes.

The mechanism was the same type as the one she had seen him hold on Wednesday, a double-coil spring, commercial grade, with a release trigger at the base of the spring plate. She had covered trap injuries in her third-year wilderness medicine rotation. She understood the mechanics. She pressed the trigger plate with both hands, held it, and said "now." He pulled the leg, and it came free. She released the plate, and the trap snapped shut on nothing.

She sat back on her heels.

He was shifting. She watched it happen, a reality her vocabulary would need a long time to catch up to. The size reduced. The fur was gone. What was left was Jace Mercer, human, lying on the ground on a cold November trail with his right hind leg pulled in close to his body, his breathing measured.

He looked at her.

"I was going to tell you tomorrow," he said.

She had known. She hadn't known the details, not the mechanism, not the word for it. But she had known for weeks that there was a truth he was moving toward, a piece of information that was the key to the architecture she had stood outside her whole life. She had been waiting with the patience of a woman who understood that some truths required the right time and the right person, and she was neither of those things for this door. He was.

"I know," she said.

She reached into the kit. She was going to look at the leg, and she was going to do this part as she did every part, with the tools she had and the information available and no room in her attention for anything that wasn't the immediate task.

He was watching her work. She could feel it.

The leg was injured, bruising already visible, probable muscle strain above the joint, and nothing she was assessing as broken. The healing rate was a topic she was going to address later, with words, in a heated cabin with a table between them and coffee, if possible. She wrapped it efficiently and sat back on her heels.

"Can you walk?"

"Yes."

"Then let's go." She stood, put the kit under her arm, and offered him her hand. He looked at it, and then he took it, and she helped him up.

"Let's get you inside."

The trail back was quiet. The cold had settled fully into

the trees. She could hear their footsteps on the frozen ground, the silence of a Montana forest at night, which wasn't silent but contained its own sounds, the creak of a branch, the small movement of life in the undergrowth, as a place with its own ongoing business. She had grown up adjacent to this. She was learning the ins and outs of it.

He didn't let go of her hand until they reached the trailhead.

She wasn't thinking about that. She was thinking about the cabin, which she knew how to find, and the coffee he would have, and the conversation she had been waiting five weeks for.

TWELVE

THE TRUTH

She drove.

He hadn't told her how to get to the cabin. She already knew the road because she had been out to BWR twice in the last week. The cabin road branched off the same access lane, so she turned onto it without asking for directions. He watched the familiar progression of pines in the headlights, said nothing, and let her be.

She drove with full attention and no wasted motion. He had noticed this about her from the beginning, a person who had trained herself to be present in whatever she was doing, and whose presence was therefore a tangible force. He felt it now from the passenger seat, her focus on the road, the weather, and him, all at once, as a trauma nurse learned to track multiple inputs without letting any one of them crowd the others.

His leg ached. He had been in worse. The joint was intact, and the muscles would resolve in a day or two, faster than they would for a human, and that speed of resolution was one of the facts he was about to have to explain.

She parked and came around to his side. He was already out, weight on the good leg until he found his footing. She clocked it and said nothing. He was grateful for that.

The cabin was dark, and he found the lights. She sat him in the kitchen chair near the table, put her kit on the table, and unwrapped the field bandaging she had done on the trail.

She worked without commentary. He sat with the patience he had for medical attention, the patience of a man who understood that the person treating him knew more about the treatment than he did and shouldn't be interrupted. She checked the joint, the range of motion, and the status of the swelling. She checked it again. She put her hand on the muscle above the joint and held it.

"This is healing faster than it should," she said. Not a question. A notation.

"Yes."

She removed her hand. Her eyes lingered on the leg for another moment and then found his face.

"So," she said.

He told her.

He'd had the planned version in his head for two weeks, the order of it, the framing, and the sequencing that would let the pieces land before he moved to the next piece. The cabin, the table, the dinner he had made, the comfort of a space he knew well and she was beginning to know. The planned version had architecture.

This version had, a kitchen chair, a first-aid kit on the table, his leg wrapped in hospital gauze he didn't own, which she had brought in a kit from the store, the two of them sharing the proximity of people who had just been through a crisis together, and no architecture at all.

He started with what they were.

Not what he was personally. What the species was, the biological fact of it, the pack structure, the centuries of what it meant to be a shifter family in a human world. He said it as he would have said it tomorrow if tomorrow had gone as planned, which was plainly, without embellishment and without minimization. These are the facts. This is what is real.

She listened. He watched her as he always watched her when she was processing; the stillness of her, Lily Thornton's attention when she was revising a significant number of her working assumptions simultaneously. She had the file open and was rewriting it. He kept talking.

"How many of you are there?" she asked.

"The Blackpine pack. Eight, not counting mates." He named them, Cole, himself, Reid, Eli, Danny, Sarah, and Old Tom. He told her about Nora, the matriarch shifter in the pack, her mate ten years dead, carrying a severed bond for a decade. He watched Lily absorb this and saw her recalculating what she had observed about Nora over the last six weeks.

"The women who come to pack dinners," she said. "Harper."

"Cole's mate. Human."

"She knows."

"She found out as you found out. She came to Blackpine investigating BWR's impossible response times." He told her about Harper, the journalist who had arrived to expose them, the woman who had ended up staying. "She's been here eight months. She knows about the pack, about what we are."

"She told me that you were a good man," Lily said. "That you'd been trying to figure out how to do this right for a while."

His eyes narrowed. "When?"

"Friday, at dinner." She held his look. "She knew what she was saying."

"She usually does."

Lily was quiet. He could see her running the Harper conversation through the new frame, understanding what Harper had been telling her, why she had said it as she had.

He told her about the mate bond. He kept it plain, the recognition, the scent, the pull that arrived involuntarily and couldn't be manufactured or faked. He told her about the claiming bite and what it did, a permanent bond, emotional sensing, and an extended lifespan. He told her what it didn't do, it didn't make a human into a shifter. Children of wolf-human pairs always came into the shift, but the mate herself remained human.

She didn't ask if he had recognized her as his mate. He understood that she was a woman who had been working from available evidence for six weeks, and that she had enough of it to have arrived at that question on her own.

She was deciding whether to ask it tonight or wait. He watched her decide.

She waited.

He went on.

The rescue operation was legitimate cover and real. Cole had taken over BWR because he needed a purpose, because a wilderness rescue operation gave the pack a reason to patrol the territory and respond to calls at speeds human teams couldn't match, and because being good at the work wasn't incompatible with using it as cover. They were good at the work. That part had always been real.

The Thorntons.

He told her about the Thorntons and watched recognition settle on her face. Not surprise. The kind of resolution that comes when you've been standing outside a building and someone opens a door you've known was there.

"Your grandparents know," he said. "Your grandfather's father knew before them. The Thorntons have been part of Blackpine's inner circle for three generations. They've known what the Mercer family is since before our father was Alpha." He paused. "They didn't tell you because we asked them not to. The pack asked them to wait until you were told by the right person at the right time. They did."

She said nothing. He watched her hold that.

"Dottie knew," she said, eventually. Not a question.

"Yes."

Her eyes dropped to her hands. He had the sense of her running an accounting, every conversation with Dottie in the past six weeks, her grandmother's answers and her silences, the words Dottie had said that now had a different architecture. He waited.

"Mrs. Patterson told me on my first day back that this town kept truths she wasn't ready to hand over. She was right. I just didn't have the key yet."

"She knew when to say it."

"Yes." Her eyes lifted to meet his. "She did."

She looked at the first-aid kit, then at the window, where the outside was the dark of two-thirty in the morning in the mountains, nothing visible but the black negative shapes of the pines against the sky.

"I've been standing just outside this my whole life," she said. Not with bitterness. Just the fact of it. "Coming back every summer, noticing details I didn't have language for. My grandmother had a trait I understood as wisdom but now see as knowledge deeper than she let on. My grandfather has always known which questions to answer and which to defer." She paused. "I left at eighteen because I didn't have the name for what I was adjacent to and didn't know how to ask for it."

"You were going to ask Earl," he said. He had seen the note in the manifest margins weeks ago. *Ask Earl about the Mercer family. When the time is right.*

"I was building up to it." Her eyes found his. "And then someone else handed me the door."

He had done that. Not as he had planned to do it. But he had gotten her here.

He told her about Amanda.

Not her face. Not her name, in a way that carried more

weight than the explanation required. He told her what had happened, a story he hadn't told anyone in full since the year it happened, when Cole had sat with him in this kitchen for four hours while Jace worked through the taxonomy of what he had done wrong and what it had cost.

He had told her badly. He had handed it to her whole, in the middle of a moment that had felt right, with no preparation and no context. She had called him a monster. He hadn't argued with her, because her fear was real and the information had no framework to land in. Her fear had been a reasonable response to an unreasonable situation that he had created by being careless about how he put the information in her hands. She had moved to Florida. Cole had managed the exposure risk.

He had spent six years understanding that the how and the when mattered as much as the what.

"I have thought about how to do it right every day since Amanda," he said. "Not obsessively. Not as a person who can't let go of a wound. More as a problem I was eventually going to have to solve, that I needed to understand before I could solve. The problem wasn't how do you tell someone you love that you are a wolf? The problem was how do you tell someone they are your mate, what that means, what it would ask of them, what it would give them and what it would cost, in a way that they have enough of who you are to hold it safely."

His eyes found hers. She was watching him.

"I was building toward that with you. Every time I came into the store. Every conversation. Every moment."

He let the word stand. "I was going to tell you Saturday. At dinner. I had the whole plan in my head, what I was going to say first, what order to say it in. I was going to build it as you built a case, as you built the picture you have in your head, piece by piece, until the name for the picture was the last piece and it had a place to land."

He stopped.

"The trap had other plans."

She said, "You still did it right."

His eyes met hers.

"You built toward it," she said. "Six weeks. Every time you came in, every conversation, every—everything." The echo was intentional, and he heard it. "I have had enough of who you are to hold it for a while now. Tonight just moved the last piece up by eighteen hours."

He watched her take that in. She had been so still, with a stillness that wasn't the stillness of someone frozen but of someone concentrating. Now her attention moved to the table, the first-aid kit, and his leg before returning to him.

"The land trust," she said. "Cole needed a purpose."

"Yes."

"My father found that."

"We know. We've been watching what he found."

She held his eyes steadily. He matched it.

"You were going to tell me," she said.

"Yes."

She was quiet. He couldn't fully read what was happening in the stillness. He had accumulated weeks of reading Lily Thornton. He had become reasonably fluent in how she communicated, but this wasn't a moment he had reference points for. He waited.

"Does it hurt?" she asked. "Shifting. Being caught in the middle of it."

He hadn't expected that question. "Yes."

She nodded. Her attention returned to his leg.

"The healing rate is going to be visible by morning," she said. "I want to look at it again when it's light."

"All right."

"And I want to see." Her eyes found his. He understood what she was asking. "Not tonight. When you're healed. When it's light, and you're not in pain. I want to see you properly."

He had built a planned version that included this moment, and in it he had offered. She was asking. He hadn't anticipated how different those two experiences would feel.

"Okay," he said.

She stood. She scanned the kitchen and found the coffeemaker without being told where it was. She had spent twelve years walking into unfamiliar rooms and locating what she needed. She made coffee.

He sat at the table and watched her move through the space he had built with his hands, and thought about how what you had long feared could resolve into an outcome entirely different from the shape the fear had given it.

She put a mug in front of him and sat back down.

"I'm staying tonight," she said. "Medical watch. Your leg."

He didn't argue. She wouldn't have accepted the argument.

They sat with their coffee in the kitchen of his cabin at two in the morning, and he told her the rest of it; the questions she had, and he answered them plainly and without embellishment. She asked about the pack bond. She asked about the claiming ceremony. She asked about what it meant for a human mate in practical terms, including lifespan and emotional sensing. She asked about Cole and Harper in a way that told him she was extrapolating from what she had observed, matching the new frame to the eight weeks of evidence she had accumulated.

"What did the pack think was going to happen?" she asked. "With me. If you didn't tell me."

"Cole was going to tell you himself." He held his mug. "He was giving me the timeline to do it my way first. He said Saturday was the limit."

She was quiet.

"He was right," she said. "Saturday was the limit." Her eyes dropped to her coffee. "I was going to ask Earl this week. I wrote it in the margins of the manifest and was going to do it."

He hadn't known that. "What were you going to ask?"

"I was going to ask him what the Mercers were." She met his eyes directly. "I think I already knew it wasn't a normal answer."

Outside, the wind moved through the pine canopy with the dry, rushing sound it made when the temperature was below freezing, a sound different from the summer sound. He had lived in this cabin long enough to know the vocabulary of weather that this building had in each season.

She set her mug down, looking down at her hands.

"I'm going to need to tell Earl," she said. "That I know. He's been carrying it for me for thirty years."

"I know."

"Not tonight."

"No. Not tonight."

Her attention drifted to the window, where the dark outside was entering the earliest stage of the hour that preceded light, not light yet, but the absence of absolute dark. He had learned to read this hour as he read most hours, as information.

She wasn't going to run. He had known this. He had known it as his wolf had known it since the first day, as it knew facts without evidence that later proved exactly right. But knowing it and having it be true in the same kitchen at three in the morning were two different kinds of knowing, and he was sitting in the second one now, with the fact of it in his hands, his chest, and his wolf, which was the quietest it had been since Amanda.

She's staying, his wolf said.

Yes.

CHAPTER

THIRTEEN

WHAT COMES NEXT

She woke to the smell of coffee and the light filtering through unfamiliar windows in the morning.

She had slept on the couch in her coat. She had meant to stay awake, monitoring the leg and the healing rate with focused attention, notes waiting to compare in the morning. At some point after four, she had been unable to sustain the monitoring and had let her eyes close. She was a nurse, not a machine, and she had also had a fairly extraordinary Friday night.

The light through the cabin windows was the pale winter-morning kind, the thin, low light of a November dawn at altitude, everything outside gray and white and still. She sat up.

He was at the stove, making coffee the same way he had made it at three in the morning, with the ease of a man in a space he had built himself, unhurried, without self-consciousness. He hadn't heard her wake up, or he had and was choosing to give her the moment to adjust.

She had come to understand this about him, that he gave people the space of their own timelines when he could. It was one of the qualities he had.

Her attention went to his leg.

He was moving on it without compensation. Not the careful, deliberate placement of a person managing an injury. The ordinary movement of a person who had an intact leg. She had wrapped and assessed that leg at eleven-thirty last night, and it had been bruised and strained and would have been on crutches for days if he had been a human patient in her ER. It was, this morning, fine.

She had seen this. She had been told this would happen. She had it in the picture now.

"You're looking at my leg," he said.

"You walked on it correctly."

"I told you it heals fast."

She logged the rate against the lore he had given her at the table last night and found it consistent. The elevated body temperature she had noted on the first day, the heat through the coat when he had caught her on the icy steps in October, went there too. She had a lot of facts to move around now that she had the framework for them.

He put a mug in front of her and sat.

She wrapped both hands around the mug. The cabin was heated. Outside, she could see the frost on the ground cover, the silver-white of early frost in low light.

"Show me," she said.

He met her eyes.

"You said when it was light and you weren't in pain," she said. "It's light. You're walking on it correctly."

He stood. He held out his hand.

She took it.

THE TREE LINE behind the cabin was pine, the cold was serious, and the light was the flat, even gray of early morning before the sun came over the ridge. She could see her breath. She had been in Blackpine long enough to have stopped noticing the cold as remarkable. It had become the medium in which the world here moved.

He walked them to a cleared area at the edge of the trees, thirty feet from the cabin. He let go of her hand.

She stood where she was. She had been in emergency medicine for six years and had prepared herself clinically, as she prepared for procedures she hadn't done before; you gathered the available information, you understood the mechanism, you kept your hands steady regardless of what happened next.

He removed his clothes without ceremony and set them on the fallen log at the clearing's edge. She noted this the way she noted clinical facts, filed it, and kept her hands steady.

He shifted.

She had seen part of this on a November forest floor ten hours ago, in the dark and in pieces and in the context of crisis. This was different. This was chosen, in the morning light, in full. She watched it happen and understood it was going to take her brain a long time to find the right vocabulary for what she was watching, because the vocabulary she had was built for a world that didn't contain this.

What was left was a wolf.

He was large, larger than any natural wolf she had ever seen or would see, and his color was the color that had been in his eyes in their most open moments, the golden-amber of late-afternoon light through honey, with cream at the chest and throat and the underside of his tail. His eyes were on her. Gold, the amber gold she had been cataloging in his human face for six weeks, the look underneath his face, and in this form it was the whole of what he was. Nothing underneath. This was it.

She didn't run.

She was aware of the part of her brain that noted the size of the animal in front of her and the distance between them and was doing a basic threat calculation. She let it run its calculation and then set it aside, because it was running on the wrong data. The data wasn't, large predator, unknown intent. The data was, six weeks of evidence, a night of conversation, and a wolf who was looking at her like a person who is staying carefully quiet because the person in front of them needs to arrive at their own pace.

She took a step forward.

He stayed still.

She took another step. She was at the edge of arm's reach. She could see the individual hairs in the fur at his shoulder, how the light caught the cream at the chest, and his stillness, which wasn't the frozen stillness of an animal choosing flight but the intentional stillness of a creature choosing presence.

She reached out and laid her hand against his shoulder.

The heat of him was remarkable. Not the wolf's fur, which was soft and thick and cold from the morning air. The heat underneath it, the elevated temperature that ran several degrees above a human baseline consistently, and that she now understood as a biological fact rather than an anomaly. She had noted it in his hands. It was present throughout.

He was still.

She stood there with her hand on his shoulder, looked at the snow on the mountains above the tree line and the pale morning sky, and let herself be in this before she needed to be anything else.

She stayed with her hand on his shoulder.

She was aware of her stillness, clinical and a quality she didn't have a medical term for. She was a nurse. She looked at situations with the trained eyes of someone who had learned that looking clearly at a truth, even a frightening one, was better than not looking. She was looking.

He looked back at her with gold eyes. He hadn't moved.

She understood that his staying there wasn't the passive watchfulness of an animal unaware of her. It was the deliberate stillness of a person choosing to let her set the pace. She had seen this in him in human form, how he had been letting her set the pace since the first day she turned and found him at the counter with his batteries.

The wolf wasn't a different creature. It was the same person.

She removed her hand, stepped back, and said, "All right."

He shifted back.

It was faster than the previous night, the transition clean and complete. He dressed without hurry, and when he looked up, she was still watching him. He stood in front of her in the cold morning light, his breath visible in the air, his hair dusted with the pine needles it had picked up from the forest floor the night before. He watched her with the expression she had learned to call the look beneath his face, the one that surfaced when he hadn't had time to arrange the surface. Except that there had been enough time, and he hadn't arranged it, and she understood that this was intentional.

Their eyes met.

"You're beautiful," she said. She meant the wolf, and she meant him, and she meant six weeks of watching a man be himself like someone who had been behind glass for a long time and had chosen, carefully and with intention, to step through it. She meant all of it, and she wasn't going to qualify any of it.

His expression shifted in a way she didn't yet have words for. She would have words for it eventually. She had time.

"The trap had other plans," she said. "You did it right. You built toward it for weeks. I had enough of you to hold it when it came." Her eyes held his. "You did everything right."

He said nothing. He was motionless in a different way than the wolf had been, like a person absorbing words he had been waiting a long time to hear.

She stepped forward and kissed him.

Not the careful almost, not the half-second where it would be easy, the one she had been standing next to for six weeks. The actual version. He had his hands at her face almost before she had fully arrived, and he kissed her back as someone who had been waiting for this for a long time and was now choosing it without reservation.

The cold was serious. Neither of them noticed it for a while.

When she stepped back, she was out of breath, his hands at her face, her body unsteady in a way that had nothing to do with the cold.

"I need to go talk to Earl," she said.

"I know."

"And then Cole."

"I know." His expression held the steadiness she had been cataloging, the whole of it now with no wall behind it. "Take the time you need."

"I will." She glanced at the mountains above the tree line, white and clear and present. Then her eyes returned to his. "Don't go anywhere."

The corner of his mouth moved. Not a full smile. The gesture of one, the one she had been cataloging for six weeks. "I'll be here," he said.

～

She drove to BWR at noon.

She had gone back to the store first, changed her clothes, told Earl she needed a few hours. He had looked at her with the expression of a man who had been expecting this for a while and was satisfied it had arrived.

"How is the leg?" he asked.

She stopped, turning to her grandfather. "You know."

"I know many things." He said it in the Thornton way, as a person who had held a secret in trust for a long time and was comfortable with that and wasn't going to perform ignorance now that the trust had been discharged. "Go."

She drove to BWR.

Cole was in the main building, at the map table, with Reid and a set of survey maps of the northern corridor and the trap placements. Reid had retrieved Jace's truck from the trailhead that morning. His attention shifted when she came in.

She said, "I know. Jace told me last night."

He studied her for three seconds with the Alpha's full assessment, and she met it without flinching. She had spent weeks in this town learning to be observed by people who knew truths she didn't yet know, and she was now a person who knew the truth.

He said, "What are you planning to do?"

"I'm not going back to Bozeman in January." She said it with the clarity of a decision already made, now needing to be stated. "I need to have a conversation with Earl and Dottie, and I need to figure out the practical shape of staying, but the decision is made."

Cole was quiet. Reid, behind him, was examining the survey maps with the focused attention of a man present in two conversations at once.

"I've been standing just outside this my whole life," she said. "I grew up in that house. I walked out of it at eighteen, without the language for what I was near, and I've spent eight years building a very good life in a place that was never quite home." She looked at Cole. "Mrs. Patterson told me on my first day back that some things go deeper than what people say out loud in this town, and I've known since that conversation that she was right. I just didn't have the key yet."

Cole held her gaze for another moment.

"Your father," he said. "He's continuing to investigate."

"I know." She had thought about this on the drive. "I'll talk to him. Not today. He's not going to stop on the basis of a phone call, but he's going to stop when I tell him directly that I know what's here, that I'm staying, and that he doesn't need to protect me from it." She paused. "My father shows his love for me through research and data, and he gets the full picture before anyone else can. When I give him my own data, he'll absorb it."

"That may take time."

"It will take time," she agreed. "He's been worrying about this for longer than I knew."

Cole looked at the map on the table, then at Reid, then back at her. He said, "The town is going to know. It already knows some of it. Marge has had you filed for three weeks."

"Marge can file me however she wants." She held his eyes. "I grew up in this town. I know how Blackpine holds secrets."

He nodded.

"Welcome home," he said.

She drove back to town.

The mountains were out above the roofline, white and clear and entirely present. She had looked at them through the store window for six weeks, feeling like someone looking at a world they were adjacent to but not inside. That wasn't how she was looking at them now.

She pulled into the lot behind the store and sat with the engine running for a minute. She had called her mother when she was twenty-two and told her she was moving to Bozeman. Her mother had said, with the directness she had, *good, you need to figure out what you actually want, not just what you think you should want.* Her mother had been right, as her mother was sometimes right about matters Lily hadn't wanted to hear.

She turned off the engine and went inside.

Earl was at the counter with his ledger. When she came in, their eyes met, and he said, in the tone of a man who had been waiting for this conversation for thirty years, "Shall I put the kettle on?"

"Yes," she said. "Please."

She sat on the stool behind the counter, watching him put the kettle on, and thought about the shape of what came next; Frank and the conversation that had to happen. Dottie, when she was ready. A clinic that didn't yet exist but would have to, eventually, because a town this far from a hospital needed one, and she was a trauma nurse who knew how to build things from scratch. She had spent years building a career in a city that was never quite home, and she had been good at it, and that was a strength she was taking with her into whatever this became.

The kettle started its work. Outside, the November mountains were white and clear. The bell above the door would ring when the next customer came in.

She was here. It had taken her eight years, a grand-mother's stroke, and a man who bought the wrong batteries to arrive at a truth that had been waiting longer than she'd known. The kettle would finish, and there would be tea, and there would be the rest of a life to get on with.

FOURTEEN

WHAT WE ARE NOW

She told Dottie on Sunday morning.

She had thought about how to do it and had concluded there was no architecture for it. She knew this from the ER. Some conversations didn't have a right approach. You sat, you said the words, and what happened after was what happened. She made two cups of tea, brought them upstairs, set one in front of her grandmother, and sat across the table.

Dottie looked at her. One look. The look that saw the thing behind the thing.

"Oh," she said.

Lily had been ready for anything except that. Not a question. No surprise. Just *oh*. The sound of a woman who had been waiting for this for a long time and had just heard the footstep she had been listening for.

"You knew," Lily said.

"I've been waiting for this conversation since you were twelve." Dottie wrapped her hands around her mug. She wasn't performing composure. She was the person she had always been, the one who understood that some truths arrived when they were ready and that the appropriate response was to receive them. "How did it happen?"

Lily told her. Not all of it. The shape of it; the weeks of building, the trap, the cabin, the morning in the clearing. The fact of the first kiss in the cold behind the tree line, with the November mountains above them.

Dottie listened. She didn't interrupt. When Lily finished, Dottie looked at the table, and Lily had the sense of watching a woman who wasn't thinking through a problem but completing a process that had been underway for thirty years.

"Earl's mother was the one who found out first," Dottie said. "Not that anyone told her. She figured it out the same way you did. She was a practical woman who paid attention, and the pieces stopped making sense any other way." Her eyes raised. "Every generation of this family has known. Not because anyone told them. Because we're people who look."

Lily thought about herself at twelve, watching the Mercer boys through the store window without knowing why she was watching, about the manifest margins, the growing list, and the years of standing adjacent to a truth she couldn't name.

"You could have told me," she said. Not with accusation. Just the fact.

"No," Dottie said. "We couldn't. The pack asked us not to. They needed it to come from the right person at the right time." She held her mug. "And I needed to know you were going to stay before I handed you a reason to fear leaving."

Lily looked at her.

"I wasn't sure you'd stay," Dottie said. "You built a good life in Bozeman. I didn't know if Blackpine was enough to pull you back." The corner of her mouth lifted. "It appears it is."

"It appears it is," Lily agreed.

Dottie reached across the table and put her hand over Lily's. Her grip was still strong. The hands of a woman who had run this store, this household, and this thirty-year secret for decades, who had done it all with grace, understanding that keeping a secret in trust required trustworthiness, not just care.

They sat like that for a while, with the tea going cold and the November light coming through the window at its low winter angle, a light that made the kitchen look like a photograph from both the past and the present at once.

"He's a good man," Dottie said eventually.

"I know."

"His father was a good man, too. The same quality. The kind that goes deep." She removed her hand and picked up her mug. "Your grandfather always said you'd end up here. I told him he was projecting."

"Were you wrong?"

"Mm," Dottie said. In the tone that meant, *I was wrong, and I knew it while I was saying it, and I am not going to give him the satisfaction of saying so directly.*

Lily smiled. Her first real one all morning.

They finished the tea. Dottie told her about the first

winter she and Earl had run the store together, in 1979, when a snowstorm closed the pass for eight days and a delivery went sideways in ways Dottie described with forensic detail, forty years of retelling and she hadn't softened any of it. Lily listened. She hadn't heard most of these stories. She hadn't been here for the winters.

She was here for this one.

SHE CALLED FRANK AT NOON.

She had thought about what to say and settled on the minimum that was true and complete, enough to ease his worry, not enough to hand him information he didn't yet have the context for. She had learned this in the ER. You gave people what they could absorb. You built toward the rest.

He answered on the second ring, as he always answered.

"Lily."

"Dad." She was at the store counter with her coffee, the store quiet on a Sunday, the cast-iron stove doing its work in the corner. Earl had gone to the hardware store. She had the building to herself. "I'm calling about the investigation."

A pause. "What about it?"

"I need you to stop."

Another pause. She could hear him recalibrating. Not with alarm. With the same quality her father had when deciding whether to comply or argue. He was a county assessor. He had spent nineteen years in the discipline of finding what people had hidden. Stopping wasn't his instinct.

"I found more," he said.

"I know. I know you found more." She kept her voice even. "I know what you found. I know what it means. I'm telling you I'm safe, I'm staying, and you don't need to protect me from this."

"You can't know what it means if you won't tell me what you know."

"Dad." She set down her coffee. "I've been here for six weeks. I've been building the same picture you have, from the inside. And I found the part you haven't found yet, which is what it's all actually for." She waited. "I'm not going to explain it to you on the phone. But I need you to trust that I looked at it clearly, made a decision, and that the decision is that I'm staying."

The silence on the other end was the silence of a man who had been operating on worry for weeks, functional anxiety, love processed through data. Now she was asking him to put the data down and trust the person instead.

"You sound different," he said.

"I feel different."

A long pause. She could hear him breathing, the sound of her father thinking.

"Are you sure?" he asked. Not "Are you safe?" Not "What did you find?" Just, "Are you sure?"

"Yes," she said. "I'm sure."

Another pause. Then, "I'm going to keep the files."

"You can keep the files."

"I'm not going to look at them."

"That's all I'm asking."

He was quiet. She waited.

"Call me Friday," he said. "The regular call."

"I will."

She hung up, sat with the phone in her hand, and looked at the store.

She had been in this store for six weeks. She had been in it before that for the summers of her childhood, every year until she was eighteen, and then in pieces for holidays, and now again for the past six weeks, in a way that was different from any of those. She had reorganized the inventory, adjusted the shelving, and learned its rhythms, and she had done all of that with the efficiency of someone good at setting up systems, but she now understood that she had been doing more than that. She had been making it hers. Building herself into the architecture of the place until the place understood she belonged.

It already knew. It had always known. She was the last to arrive at what the store, the town, her grandfather, and her grandmother had understood for years.

The cast-iron stove ticked in the corner. The light through the front window was the low, flat gray of a November Sunday, the mountains barely visible through a high, thin overcast. She had learned to read both the way she learned to read everything in Blackpine, as information, as the vocabulary of a place that spoke in its own language.

She picked up her coffee and went back to work.

Dottie came downstairs at two, moving with the

careful ease of a woman who had been told to rest, had rested, and was now done with it. Her eyes swept across Lily behind the counter, then the store, then Lily's presence in it, which was different from how it had been when she arrived six weeks ago.

"How did it go with your father?" she asked.

"He'll be all right."

"He always is." Dottie settled into the chair behind the counter, the one that had been behind the counter for as long as Lily could remember. "He loves badly, your father. The Thornton men tend to. Your grandfather did too, for a while, before he figured out another way." She picked up her book. "Frank will figure it out."

"I know."

"How did he leave it?" Dottie asked.

Lily thought about her father's last question, not *"are you safe?"* or *"what did you find?"* but *"are you sure?"* It was the question of a man who had stopped trying to manage the outcome and was just asking about her. "He asked if I was sure."

"That's his version of the real question," Dottie said. "For him, that's as close as he gets."

"I know," Lily said.

Dottie opened her book. Outside, the November sky had gone the flat white of a day that wasn't going to improve, the mountains invisible behind it. Inside, the stove ticked, and the floor creaked in the places it always creaked, and the store held its smell of wood and dust and decades of the same family running the same building.

It was already hers. It had been for a long time.

ON MONDAY, she went to BWR as someone who belonged there.

The distinction wasn't in what she did upon arrival. It was in how she carried herself going in, walking through a door that was open for you, rather than one you were uncertain about. She had been to BWR half a dozen times. This was the first time she arrived without the ambient awareness of being a visitor.

Cole was at the map table. He looked up when she came in, and he gave her the nod he gave the pack, brief, acknowledging, assuming she was where she was supposed to be.

She pulled up a chair.

He walked her through it the way he walked the pack through things, direct, no unnecessary softening. What was the role? What it wasn't. Not official. Not paid. Not a clinic. The pack had no doctor, no vet who could ask the right questions, no formal medical infrastructure. What they had was the knowledge that the human medical system couldn't account for what they were, and that eventually someone would get hurt badly enough to need someone who could.

"You're a trauma nurse," he said. "You've spent six years in emergency medicine. You know how to work without resources, and you know how to keep your mouth shut." He didn't look away. "That's what this is."

"I understand."

"If you see an injury you can't explain medically, you tell Jace or me. You don't speculate outside the pack."

"I understand."

"If you're ever uncertain about whether a case is pack business or human medicine, you err toward pack business."

"Yes."

He was quiet, studying her with the Alpha's assessment, the one that searched for the thing underneath what people said. She held that gaze without flinching. She had been observed by that quality from various angles for weeks, and she had stopped finding it unsettling around week four.

"Harper," he said.

"What about her?"

"She didn't know what she was walking into when she got here. She found out, and she chose to stay." He said it without comparison, just the fact of it. "You're different. You grew up adjacent to this. You had more time to see it before you chose." His eyes held hers steadily. "What I'm saying is, I know you understand what you're agreeing to."

"I know," Lily said. "I've been agreeing to it since I was twelve. I just didn't have the language."

His expression changed. No surprise. The look of a man who had been Alpha for long enough to recognize when someone was exactly what the pack needed and when they had always been.

"Welcome to BWR," he said.

She stayed for three hours. She went through the medical supplies they had, assessed what they were missing, and wrote a list she would fill through a professional medical supplier, ordered under her nursing credentials. The gaps were significant; she found two expired tourniquets, a blood pressure cuff she didn't trust, no suture kit, and an antibiotic stock that would have been inadequate for a human patient and was certainly inadequate for a pack member whose immune response ran at a different pace. She made the list methodically, as she had in the ER when she was taking over a crash cart, no editorializing, just what was there and what wasn't.

She talked through the existing protocols with Jace, who had been handling minor field injuries for twelve years with the improvised competence of a man who had learned what he needed and nothing more. He knew pressure and stitching and when to hold still and let the shifter healing do the work. He didn't know the things she knew, which made the combination useful. She asked questions. He answered them.

When she left, she drove back to town with the feeling of a woman who had done the right thing and knew it.

Not the feeling of having made a decision. Those she knew; she had made a great many decisions in the last six weeks, each one incremental, each one accumulating weight. This was different. This was the feeling of having arrived somewhere she had been heading for a long time without knowing the address.

The mountains came back into view as she cleared the last curve before town, white and sharp above the tree line, doing what they always did, being there. She had looked at these mountains through the store window for six weeks from the wrong side of a truth she couldn't name. She was on the right side of it now.

She parked behind the store and went in through the back.

Earl was behind the counter. When she came in, their eyes met, his holding seventy-three years of watching Blackpine and seeing most of what it contained.

"How'd it go?" he asked.

"Good," she said. "Both of them."

He made a sound that wasn't quite *mm*. Warmer than that. The sound of a man who had been running a long patience and could feel it resolving.

She went behind the counter, and they opened the store. A few minutes later, the bell shrieked, and Mrs. Patterson came in for her weekly supplements. Lily answered her questions, listened to her news about the water tower, and wrote down the name she was given for the Whitefish pharmacy. The store settled into the rhythm of a Monday in November, and that was that.

CHAPTER

FIFTEEN

DAMAGE

Sarah came back from Tuesday's northern patrol, shaking.

Not the cold-induced shaking Cole knew, a different quality. This was internal. The vibration of a body running a temperature and not knowing what to do with it, a deep muscular tremor, her system working hard on a threat it couldn't identify.

He had her stop on the HQ steps and put a hand to her forehead before she could say anything about not needing a fuss.

"How long?"

"Started on the trail. Two hours ago, maybe three." She was holding herself with the controlled steadiness of a woman who had been running field operations for twelve years and wasn't going to let a fever unsettle her. "I've had worse."

"You haven't had worse in six years."

"The flu of 2020 was significantly worse."

"That was different." He moved inside and let her follow, which she did at her own pace. She wasn't catastrophically ill. She was clearly not well. The temperature was running high. He could feel it from a foot away, the elevated heat of a shifter body in response mode, which he had learned, as Alpha, to read as information.

He watched her sit down at the long table with the care of someone managing their own weight carefully, and pulled out his phone.

Jace picked up on the second ring.

"Sarah's back from the northern run. Running a fever. Not an emergency, but I want Lily to look at her when she's in."

A pause. "How high?"

"High enough that I'm calling."

"I'll let her know."

Cole put the phone down, got a glass of water, and set it in front of Sarah, who accepted it without protest. He sat across from her.

"What did you run through?" he asked.

"The standard corridor. Mile three to six, eastern edge, back through the creek crossing." She drank the water. "Same route as last week."

He noted it. The same route as last week meant the same route as the trap corridor, which he'd been watching closely. Two separate facts could be unrelated. He wasn't going to assume they were.

The fever peaked on Wednesday and broke by

Thursday morning. Sarah slept through most of it, which was the correct response. Characteristically, she refused the offer of the infirmary cot and instead took over the long couch in the common room with the territorial ease of a field scout who had evaluated her options and chosen the one with the best sightlines. Cole had looked in twice. Both times, she had been asleep. Both times, her color had been better than before.

She was back on her feet Thursday afternoon, with the recovered spirit of a body that had run a hard process and completed it. She came to the table at four with coffee and a look that made it clear the episode was concluded and she preferred not to discuss it further. Cole didn't press her. He noted her recovered temperature, her improved color, and the return of her standard watchfulness. She was fine.

Cole had spent Wednesday watching. Not over Sarah, who needed rest and privacy and had both, but over the patterns. There was a quality to Wednesday at HQ when a pack member was down, a low-grade collective attention, the pack bond running at a slightly elevated pitch, everyone in range more alert than usual without discussing it. Harper had asked him once if the pack always knew when someone was hurt. He had said yes, approximately. She had asked what approximately meant. He had said, not the specifics, but the direction of things. You knew a matter needed attending to. You didn't always know what. He reviewed the boundary camera feeds from the northern corridor. He went over Reid's trap placement map for the fourth time. He considered the three traps and the progression of their placement, trail, off-trail, anticipated movement zone, and the person who had been thoughtful enough to iterate.

A presence was operating in the northern corridor with a purpose. The traps weren't random. The placement had logic. He didn't have enough information to name the purpose yet, but the pattern was there, and he wasn't going to stop watching it.

What he had was a wolf who had run the same corridor and come back sick.

Cole wasn't going to assume fine meant nothing.

She got Jace's call Tuesday afternoon and drove out to BWR before closing.

She had been waiting for this, as nurses do for the first real use of a new role, not wanting anyone to be hurt, but understanding that the role has no meaning until it is needed. She had begun learning the medical particulars of treating a body that healed at a shifter's rate, faster than any protocol she had been trained in, faster than the standard recovery windows, fast in ways that would read as impossible on any chart she'd ever filled out.

The role had been waiting for her. It turned out she had been waiting for the role.

Sarah Redhawk sat at the long table with a glass of water and the contained expression of someone managing an inconvenience rather than an illness. She was tall, athletic, dark-haired, with the physical presence that Lily had started recognizing in the pack members as distinct from ordinary human presence. A quality in how they occupied space, a density to it that she understood now as biology rather than personality.

"I hear you caught a bug," Lily said.

"I catch things occasionally. It passes."

"Let me see."

Sarah extended her arm, mild, unbothered, compliant because refusal would require more effort. Lily took her wrist. Pulse fast but not alarmingly so. Temperature already perceptible from contact, elevated, though the number was harder to determine without a thermometer calibrated for shifter baseline.

"Do you have a thermometer here?" she asked Jace, who was leaning against the kitchen doorframe with the presence of a man who was there without hovering.

"Closet, first shelf."

She got it. Took the temperature. The number was high but not outside what she was beginning to understand as the pack's normal range of response to illness. Their baselines ran elevated, and their fevers ran higher relative to that baseline than a human's would. She made a note of the number and logged it.

"Any localized pain? Headache, joint pain, respiratory symptoms?"

"No. No. No."

"Nausea? Visual changes?"

"No."

"When did it start?"

"Mid-patrol, around the three-mile mark. Onset was fast. I went from fine to this in under an hour."

Lily noted that. Onset in under an hour was fast. Fast for a human, fast for a shifter. The pack bond gave them resilience and a heightened immune response, but it didn't make them immune to illness, nor did it slow the onset of pathogens that moved quickly through their systems.

"Where were you running?" she asked.

"Northern corridor. Mile three to six, east side."

She wrote it down in the small notebook she had started keeping. Not formal medical records. She didn't have the infrastructure for them and couldn't create them without raising questions she wasn't equipped to answer yet. Just notes. Observations. The kind of running documentation she had kept in the ER when a case was still developing and the full picture wasn't yet available.

Northern corridor, miles 3–6, east side. Onset under one hour. Fever, no other symptoms. Resolution: pending.

She studied what she had written. Her attention fixed on the location.

She had heard that location before. She had heard it from Jace, in connection with the traps.

She didn't say anything. She was a nurse. She knew the difference between the data she had and the connection she was inferring. A single fever in a single pack member after that patrol route wasn't a pattern. That was a data point. You needed at least three before you started calling it a pattern, and she had one.

She noted it.

She had been doing this since her first week in the ER, keeping the case open on things that didn't fully resolve. The attending had told her in her second month that the ability to hold uncertainty without prematurely closing it was one of the most important skills in emergency medicine. Most people wanted the diagnosis. They wanted the file closed. They wanted to know the diagnosis so they could deal with it. The people who were good at this work were the ones who could sit with *not yet* and not reach for a conclusion just to have one.

She had been doing this since her first year in the ER. She was good at it. She updated her note.

Northern corridor, miles 3–6, east side. Onset under one hour. Fever, no other symptoms. Rapid resolution. No secondaries.

Not yet. But she was keeping it. She closed the notebook and put it in her bag. Her look returned to Sarah, who was watching her with the expression of a woman who had been assessed by many people over the years and had developed a practiced patience for it. Lily had the sense that Sarah Redhawk was filing her too, running her own assessment, reaching her own conclusions, keeping them to herself with practiced ease.

They would understand each other, Lily thought. It might take a while. But the shape of the understanding was already there.

"Rest today and tomorrow," she said. "Fluids. If the fever spikes above what I just got, let Cole know and he'll get word to me. If it breaks on its own, which it probably will, let me know when it does."

Sarah nodded, unsurprised.

"I'll check back Thursday," Lily said.

Driving back to town, she went over what she had. One data point. One location. One fever with an unusual onset profile in a body that wasn't human but that she was learning to read as she had learned to read anything, systematically and without rushing to the conclusion.

She had been in emergency medicine long enough to know that the cases that mattered were the ones that didn't fit. The obvious cases diagnosed themselves. The interesting ones were the ones where the standard framework didn't cover everything, where you had to hold the anomaly open and keep adding data until the picture clarified.

She had one anomaly. She was holding it open.

The northern range, white at the top, the arrangement of peaks she knew now. Somewhere in that range, in the corridor between the third- and sixth-mile markers on the eastern boundary trail, a process had happened to Sarah Redhawk that Lily didn't yet have a name for.

She stored it, and kept driving, and didn't draw a line she didn't have the evidence to draw. That was the discipline. That was what the work had always required of her.

THE FEVER BROKE THURSDAY MORNING, as he had expected. Sarah was at the table at six-thirty with coffee, her expression that of a woman who had processed the illness and was done with it. Cole didn't tell her she seemed better. She knew she was better. He called Jace. Jace would call Lily.

He sat across from her with his coffee and the map of the northern corridor that had been lying on the map table, Reid's annotations in their precise hand marking the trap placements, the patrol routes, the dead zones.

He turned his attention to the eastern edge of the miles-three-to-six stretch.

On the second trap Reid had marked.

On the probable zone for a third placement Reid had marked.

Where Sarah had been running on Tuesday.

The overlap was significant. He didn't know what it meant. Two data points that shared a location weren't a pattern. They were a coincidence, and coincidences needed a third point before they became a pattern worth acting on. He was going to wait for the third point.

He was also going to make sure Lily's note about Sarah's patrol route had been recorded somewhere he could find it again.

Northern corridor, miles three to six. Same as the traps. He didn't know what the traps and the fever had in common. He knew they had the location in common.

He rolled up the map, put it back in the tube, and went to find Reid.

Reid was at the workbench, doing what he did, maintenance work, precise and requiring attention. He looked up as Cole came in, waiting. Reid always waited. Information arrived when it was ready, and he had made his peace with that a long time ago.

"Sarah's clear," Cole said.

"I know. I could feel it."

"I want a second sweep of miles three to six. Eastern edge. This time look for anything that doesn't fit. Not just traps. Anything that looks like it was placed, not natural."

Reid looked at him with the quality he got when he was running a calculation in parallel. "The fever."

"I don't know yet. I want to know."

Reid set down his tool. "I'll go out Friday morning."

"Before dawn."

"Before dawn," Reid confirmed.

Cole went back to the map table. He set his coffee down and looked at the northern corridor once more, at the miles where Sarah had run and where the traps had been set, and at the space between those two facts that still lacked a name.

The space was what mattered. Not the individual points, but the space between them. He had been an Alpha long enough to learn that the pattern you were looking for was usually in the gap, not in the point. He was watching the gap.

He had also been carrying this pack long enough to know that the instinct that said *pay attention* was worth trusting even when the data was thin. The fever had been short. Sarah had recovered. There had been no new traps finds since the Friday incident. There was nothing to act on, not yet. But the instinct didn't require action. It required attention, which he was giving it.

Jace had mentioned Tuesday evening that Lily had asked where Sarah ran without being prompted and had written it down. He made a mental list of what he knew, the trap corridor, the fever, the timing, and the fact that Lily had noted the location without being told to. The location. Always the same location. The eastern edge, miles three to six. That was the consistent factor across all three data points; the traps, the fever, the patrol route. Three separate data points, same geography. Not proof. But an accumulation that warranted watching.

He was going to find out what it was. He had always been better at keeping questions open than forcing answers. That was the truth about carrying the pack. You had to know when to push and when to watch. Right now he was watching.

The coffee had gone cold. He drank it anyway. Outside, the November dark sat at the windows. The territory was out there, running its own quiet business, holding what it held. He let it.

Reid came back a few minutes later with his empty mug and set it in the sink. He didn't say anything. His eyes swept the map once, noting where Cole was focused, and he left the room. That was Reid. He didn't crowd a thought you were working through. Cole had always been grateful for that quality. He was grateful for it now.

The building settled into its night sounds. The stove ticked. The equipment room was dark. Somewhere in the northern corridor, the territory was doing what territory did, persisting, holding, keeping its own record of what moved through it. Cole added his attention to that record and went to bed.

SIXTEEN

THE STRANGER

Reid went out Friday morning before dawn. Jace went with him.

He hadn't been asked. He had offered on Thursday evening, when Cole briefed the pack on the second sweep request, and Cole had given him the nod that meant *your call* without meaning it was necessary. It wasn't necessary. Reid was the pack's best tracker and didn't need company to execute a methodical sweep of a corridor he had already mapped twice. He also didn't refuse company when it was offered with the right understanding, that Jace wouldn't get in the way, would hold his wolf quiet, and would let Reid do the work. Reid had not mentioned the previous weekend. Jace had not offered an explanation.

Jace had his own reasons for going. He had been thinking about Lily since Thursday, since Cole had said the fever broke and Sarah was clear, with the quality he had when he was satisfied and concerned simultaneously.

Jace had run the math on what Lily had noted, what Cole had noted, and what they both were holding open.

He was thinking about her as he had been for two months, with the full clarity of a man who had stopped managing the thinking. She was part of the pack's life now, which meant she was part of this. The northern corridor wasn't abstract anymore. It was where she had driven on a Wednesday afternoon to see the reality of it. It was where she had held a trap and asked the right questions. It was where Sarah had run and come back sick.

He wanted to understand the territory as she would need to understand it. He wanted to be able to explain it to her. The northern corridor. The location where the traps had been placed. The location where Sarah had run and come back sick. Reid had found a chemical residue in the ground at mile four that Cole had asked Lily to assess. He wanted to know what he was asking her to assess.

He wanted to see the corridor himself, at this hour, in wolf form, with Reid.

They went out in the dark.

REID RAN the sweep with the methodical patience of a man who had tracked things in the dark for eighteen years and had long since stopped finding it demanding. He moved through the corridor just below wolf speed, slower than he could go but fast enough that Jace had to maintain focus to keep up. Not a challenge. An invitation to be present.

The corridor between miles three and six was familiar to Jace in the abstract, the boundary map he had reviewed a hundred times, the camera feed positions, the general topology. It was different in wolf form at four in the morning, with the ground frozen and the snow between the trees catching the ambient light, while the layered information of smell arrived in waves as they moved through it. He had run this corridor in human form, in daylight, with equipment. This was the version that mattered.

Reid stopped at mile four.

He stopped like a wolf who has caught a scent that doesn't fit, and Jace recognized the response. He went still, let his wolf's nose work, and waited.

There was a chemical trace in the ground.

Not a trap. Not metal. The scent was different from the commercial steel of the leg-hold mechanisms they had found. This was older, a compound that had been here long enough to settle into the soil rather than sit on top of it. Chemical. Faint. The faintness of a substance that had diluted over time rather than one that wasn't there.

Reid moved in a slow circle, methodical, nose down. He stopped twice. Jace watched him work.

When Reid shifted back to human, he did it efficiently, barely pausing, and dressed from the cache at the boulder shelf without comment. Jace shifted and joined him.

"Not a trap," Jace said.

"No." Reid crouched and pressed his fingers into the snow layer at the base of a fallen log. He didn't disturb it. Just contact, reading it. "A substance was here. Not recently. Months, maybe. A compound that went into the soil."

Jace looked at the log. At the ground around it. It looked like a forest floor in November. It looked like nothing.

"What kind of compound?"

Reid looked up at him. "I don't know yet. I need to get Cole."

They moved east on foot, continuing the sweep in human form. The corridor in wolf form had been different from the corridor on any map—richer, more layered, the ground holding pressure underfoot in a way that no map could capture. He had run this corridor hundreds of times. He was seeing it differently tonight, with Reid's attention shaping his own, looking for the thing underneath the thing.

The mile-four chemical residue was in his nose. The cold wasn't dissipating as it usually did. It was a compound that had penetrated deep into the soil and remained there. He noted this and kept moving.

Reid stopped first at a rock outcropping at mile five. It looked natural from a distance. It wasn't. An exterior position, oriented to watch movement along the corridor approach, built into the rock face with the same professional patience as everything else they had found out here. Reid examined it without touching it. He photographed it.

They moved on.

Reid found the observation blind at mile five and a half.

It was professional, weatherproofed, sightlines carefully selected, braced against the rock face in a way that would survive a Montana winter. Oriented inward, toward the interior of pack territory, not toward the corridor edge.

Not watching what entered the territory. Watching what happened inside it.

Jace stood in front of it and felt his wolf go completely still. This wasn't a hunter's position. A hunter needed to see what was coming toward them. This was a position built by someone who wanted to see what the territory's occupants did when they thought they weren't being watched. The distinction mattered.

"How long?" he asked.

Reid ran his fingers along the frame of the structure, reading it as he read everything. "At least six weeks. Possibly longer."

Six weeks.

Lily had arrived six weeks ago.

He didn't voice the connection out loud because it wasn't yet a connection. It was a coincidence of timing, and coincidences required corroboration before they became connections. But his wolf noted it with the alertness of an instinct that had been assessing threats since the moment Lily Thornton became relevant to their lives.

The first blind was outside, watching the corridor. This one was inside, watching the territory. Two blind spots. Two positions. Both professional. Both patient.

Someone had been watching them for six weeks.

Reid went through the blind with the methodical care he brought to everything. He photographed the construction without touching it. He mapped the sightlines, noting what was visible from this position; the access road, the eastern approach to the HQ clearing, and a section of the boundary trail that pack members used regularly. He worked silently, as he always did, with the concentration of a man building an evidence file in his head.

Jace stayed back and let him work. His job was to watch the perimeter while Reid documented, which he did with his wolf running at full attention, alert to any sound or scent that might indicate they weren't alone. The forest in November was quiet. The cold held sound in its own way. If anyone was watching them now, they were doing it from a distance Jace couldn't detect.

When Reid finished, he stepped back from the blind without disturbing it.

"We leave it," he said. It wasn't a question.

"We leave it," Jace confirmed. "Cole's call on what happens next."

THEY REPORTED to Cole at six-thirty. Cole was at the map table with coffee, a man who had been awake for a while and had settled into waiting. He had known they were coming back; the pack bond told him direction and general state, and the general state of both of them had been focused-and-returning since before first light.

Cole listened without expression. He studied the photographs Reid had taken with the compressed intensity of a man absorbing information he had been anticipating and didn't want to be right about.

"Two separate operations," Cole said.

"Three," Reid said. "The traps. The corridor blind. This blind. Three distinct positions, three distinct purposes." He set the photographs on the table. "The traps are surveillance by proxy. What the trap catches tells you what uses the territory. The corridor blind watches movement. The interior blind watches behavior. Someone is building a picture of this territory."

Jace listened without adding commentary. This was Cole and Reid's conversation to have; they were the ones who ran operations and tracked threats. His role was to carry the information forward, to be the conduit between what the pack knew and what Lily needed to know. He would do that well.

"How long before they know we've found the blinds?" Cole asked.

"Unknown. If they're checking the positions regularly, they'll notice our scent. If they're monitoring remotely, they may not know until they visit again." Reid paused. "Either way, we've changed the parameters. They know they're not invisible anymore."

Cole was quiet after that. He looked at the photographs Reid had laid out, the exterior sightline post, the interior watching position, and the ground disturbance at mile four. Three distinct elements, each with a distinct purpose, assembled over the same six weeks. Whoever was building this picture of the territory was patient and systematic.

"Good," Cole said. "Let them know."

"The chemical in the ground near mile four," he said.

"I want Lily to look at it," Reid said. "Or at least at a sample. I don't know what it is. She might recognize the parameters of what category it falls into, even if she can't identify the compound."

"Without a lab."

"She's a trauma nurse. She's done field assessments without equipment before."

Cole was quiet. Jace watched him work through it, the Alpha's read on the information he was putting into a larger frame than what was visible in this room. Twelve years of carrying this pack's safety had given Cole a quality: when threat information came in, he went still. Not frightened. Contained. The stillness of a man calculating the severity of a threat before he allowed himself to react to it.

"Don't confront anything," Cole said. "Either position. Don't alter anything. Don't let whoever it is know we found them."

"Already maintained," Reid said.

"I want a perimeter around the interior blind. Forty-foot radius. Anyone in the pack runs outside that radius until I say otherwise." He picked up his coffee. "And I want to know what's in that ground at mile four."

His attention shifted to Jace. The message was clear. *You know what you need to do.*

JACE TOLD LILY THAT EVENING.

He found her at the store after closing, the quiet hour

when the front was locked and the back was warm from the day's heat. She was going through the weekly accounts at the counter. He knocked on the back door. She let him in.

She could tell from his face that it was serious. She didn't ask. She set down the accounts and waited.

He told her plainly, as he told her things now, without the management layer. What Reid had found; the second blind, the interior position, the estimated six weeks. The chemical compound in the ground at mile four. Its presence without identification, the fact of it.

She listened. She had the quality she got when she was taking in information that required action rather than reassurance, fully present, hands quiet, the filing happening in real time.

"Six weeks," she said when he finished.

"At least."

"That's when I arrived."

He kept his eyes on her. "It may be coincidence."

"May be." Her attention drifted to the far wall, to the organizational chart she had put up in her first week, the inventory system she had built. She studied it as she studied data. "You think someone is watching the pack."

"Someone has been watching the territory. Whether they know what the pack is, I don't know. Whether they're watching the territory because of what the pack is, I don't know."

"Are they watching the wolves or the people?"

He had known she would ask that. "We don't know yet."

She absorbed this. The silence stretched, but he had learned to read it. Lily Thornton deciding what to do with new information. Not distressed. Updating.

"The mile four compound," she said. "You want me to look at it."

"Cole does. Reid does." His eyes met hers. "I do."

"Can you get me a soil sample without disturbing the area?"

"Reid can. He can take it without leaving any evidence he was there."

"Then yes." Her eyes held his. "This is what I'm here for."

He understood what she meant. Not just the medical skills. The whole of it, a combination of training and discretion and the willingness to look at things clearly that made her the person who could stand in the middle of what the pack was and ask the right questions without flinching from the answers.

He had known this about her since the first day. He was arriving at the full shape of it.

"I'll have Reid go back tomorrow," he said.

"Good." She went back to the accounts. He stayed leaning against the counter, at ease in a space where they were allowed to just be.

"Are you staying?" she asked, without looking up.

"For a while," he said.

She nodded and kept working, and he made himself useful by refilling the cast-iron stove from the basket by the wall, checking the door seal that had been sticking, and sorting the stack of supplier invoices that had accumulated on the counter where Earl put things he intended to deal with later. The store had its own rhythms when it was closed. He was learning them, which was another way of saying he was learning her, which was another way of saying he was doing what his wolf had been doing since the first day, now with his whole self instead of the parts he had allowed before.

They stayed like that for an hour in the quiet of the closed store, one of the better hours he had had in recent memory. At some point, her attention lifted from the accounts and found him watching her. She didn't turn away, and the connection between them that had been building since October was there, acknowledged, present.

"Saturday," she said.

"What about it?"

"Come for dinner. Dottie's cooking."

He smiled. It wasn't his charming smile. It was the one that had no performance in it at all. "All right."

"All right," she said, and went back to the accounts, and he stayed until the stove had gone through another cycle, and then he drove back to BWR with the quiet of a man who had somewhere to be and someone to be there with.

The road out of town was dark. The mountains were invisible against the night sky, present only as the absence of stars. He drove with the windows cracked to let in the cold, which he liked, and thought about the three operations Reid had mapped, traps, corridor blind, interior blind. Someone was watching. The pack was being watched.

But the pack was also watching back now. And the pack had an advantage the watcher didn't know about. They had a woman who could read medical data and biological patterns, who could look at a soil sample and begin to understand what had been put into the ground.

The watcher had been invisible for six weeks. That was over now. The pack knew they were being watched and what kind of watching it was, professional, patient, sustained. The balance had shifted, and the pack was on the right side of it.

CHAPTER

SEVENTEEN

THE ROGUE

The pack bond sensed him on Saturday morning, other, the same, wrong.

Cole felt it as he felt anything that touched the bond's edge, not loudly but with the clarity of a signal that was unambiguous about its nature even when it was ambiguous about its meaning. A wolf. Male. No pack signature attached to him, no resonance of belonging. The bond knew what belonged to Blackpine and what didn't, and this wasn't Blackpine, but it wasn't nothing. It was a wolf who had once had a pack and no longer did.

He was at HQ within twenty minutes. Reid was already there.

"How far?"

"Eastern boundary. Moving slowly. Not running." Reid had his coat on and the maps already out. "He's been on the move for a while. The trail is old."

"Injured?"

"Not physically. The other kind."

Cole knew what he meant. He had seen it once before, in the Oregon pack elder who had come through Blackpine years before Old Tom had joined them, the last survivor of a pack dissolution. There was a kind of damage that came from extended solitary existence in a shifter; the systems designed for connection operating without connection, the wolf bond running without a pack to run it into. It didn't break a person quickly. It broke them slowly, in ways that were hard to see from the outside until they were far along.

"How far along?" he asked.

"Far enough that I'm not comfortable leaving him on the territory unattended."

Cole picked up his phone and sent the same message to every pack member.

> Pack meeting, HQ, one hour. Non-negotiable.

He had called emergency meetings before. Twice for territory disputes, once for the situation with the logging company two years ago, and once when Old Tom had a cardiac episode and the pack needed to know what was happening and what to do. This was different from any of those. This was the pack being asked to make a decision that would define who they were, one they couldn't take back.

He went to the window and looked out at the eastern tree line. Somewhere in that direction, moving slowly, the lone wolf was coming. He wasn't hunting, not fleeing, not doing anything with obvious intent. He moved, as a body moves when it has been in motion for too long and no longer remembers any other way to be.

Cole knew what that looked like. Once, before he was Alpha, in a woman who had come through the territory alone. She had been further gone than this one. She hadn't stayed. He had been nineteen years old and had watched his father make the decision to let her pass through, and he had never forgotten the look in her eyes.

He wouldn't forget this one either, whatever happened next.

THEY CAME in one at a time over the next forty minutes, Jace, then Nora, then Danny, then Eli, then Sarah, then Old Tom, who came last and unhurried because Old Tom's relationship with urgency had always been philosophical. Reid had the maps out. Cole stood at the end of the table.

He told them what Reid had found. A lone male shifter, no pack, several days on pack territory, moving east. Unstable. Not dangerous, not yet, but on a trajectory that would become dangerous if left unaddressed.

"How unstable?" Danny asked.

"Shifting involuntarily. Not eating," Reid said. "I tracked him for two miles. He shifted twice without apparent intent and didn't seem aware he'd done it."

Danny absorbed this. The pack absorbed this.

Old Tom was the first one to speak. He had the wisdom of an elder who had been alive long enough to have opinions that weren't theoretical. "A wolf without a pack doesn't last," he said. "You know what becomes of them."

"I know," Cole said.

"So what's the question?"

"The question is whether we bring him in or drive him out. I won't do either without the pack's agreement."

The table was quiet. Jace watched Cole with the full attention he gave when reading the Alpha's true position beneath what was offered as a question. Cole let him look. He wasn't trying to hide his position. He was trying to give the pack genuine agency in a decision that would have consequences either way.

Nora said, "What happens if we drive him out?"

"He keeps moving. He deteriorates. Somewhere else, someone else makes this decision. Or no one does." Cole looked at her. "That's the honest answer."

"And if we bring him in?"

"We hold him for a day or two. Let the pack bond stabilize him. Give him a chance to be a person instead of just a wolf. And then he makes his own choice about where he goes next." He paused. "He won't stay. Reid says he can't, and I believe Reid. This isn't a permanent addition. This is a decision about what kind of pack we are."

More quiet.

"Bring him in," Jace said.

The rest followed. Reid, without inflection. Nora, with the nod she gave when a decision was made correctly. Danny, who found the whole situation both concerning and interesting. Eli, who said "obviously" with the confidence of someone who hadn't been alive long enough to find these decisions complicated. Sarah, whose input was "Yes." Old Tom, last, who said nothing but looked at Cole with the expression that meant, *I knew what you were going to say before you said it.*

"Bring him in," Cole said.

The decision settled into the room, collective and final. Cole looked at each of them, his brother, who had spoken first; Reid, who tracked everything and trusted Cole's read; Nora, who ran the household operations and understood what bringing someone in would mean for the space's physical logistics; Danny, whose mind was already running scenarios; Sarah, who had said one word and meant the world in it; Old Tom, who had been alive long enough to know what this decision would cost and what it would buy.

This was what a pack was. Not just the bonds, the territory, or the blood. It was the decision made together, owned together. Whatever came next belonged to all of them.

SHE WAS at the store Saturday when Jace called.

Not about the soil sample, which Reid had told her he would collect in the morning. About a person at BWR who needed medical assessment. Jace said it in the careful way he used when the situation was unusual and he didn't want to alarm her before she had seen it for herself.

She drove out.

The man was in the common room, seated at the long

table, and he was clearly not fine. He was somewhere in his thirties, dark-haired, with a physical frame that suggested past strength, now being lost for a while. He was in human form and holding it with the visible effort of a person gripping a wet rope. His eyes tracked her when she came in, hypervigilant, his threat assessment running continuously for a long time.

She had seen this before. Not in shifters. In the ER, in patients who had come in after extended exposure to extreme stress, the body that no longer knew how to stop preparing for the worst, the eyes that couldn't finish a sweep, the stillness that wasn't rest but tactical positioning. She knew what she was looking at.

Cole was at the far end of the room, not crowding the table. She understood the distance, giving the man space, giving her room to work. She pulled up the chair across from the man, not next to him, not looming over him. Level. Non-threatening.

"My name is Lily," she said. "I'm a nurse."

He looked at her. The look took a full second to arrive. "Owen."

"Owen." She nodded. "Cole asked me to come take a look at you. I'm not going to do anything you don't agree to. Can I check your pulse and temperature?"

A pause. "Yes."

She worked through the assessment the same way she had with Sarah, except this was different in quality from Sarah's acute illness. Sarah's fever had been the body's response to an external pathogen. Owen's elevated temperature was different, the thermal signature of a wolf form that kept wanting to assert itself through the human one, the shift and counter-shift running just below the surface and generating heat as a byproduct.

She noted everything. She didn't ask him to explain any of it. She had learned in six years of emergency medicine that the most useful thing you could do for someone in extreme distress was to address the physical reality and let the narrative come in its own time.

"When did you last eat?" she asked.

"I don't remember."

"Day before yesterday? Further back?"

"Further back."

She went to the kitchen and made a sandwich, the simple architecture of a task that required no decisions. She brought it back and set it in front of him without ceremony.

He looked at it, then picked it up and ate. She watched him without speaking, as she would have watched a patient in the ER who needed space more than conversation. The mechanics of eating were familiar to him; that much was clear. The mechanics of being fed by another person weren't. He kept glancing at her between bites, as if checking that the situation was still what it appeared to be. She stayed where she was, didn't move closer, and didn't fill the silence. Silence had different textures, and some of them were necessary. It wasn't her job to remove them.

When he had finished, she asked, "Is there anything specific you need me to look at? Any pain, any injury?"

"No."

"All right." She folded her hands on the table. "Cole is going to let you rest here for a couple of days. I'll come by tomorrow. If anything changes overnight, Jace has my number."

He looked at her with the air of a man used to things changing, and not for the better. "Why," he said.

She understood the question. Not *why come by,* but *why any of this?* Why take him in? Why feed him? Why the hospitality of people who didn't have to offer it.

"Because you needed somewhere to stop," she said. "And this is where you stopped."

He held this. She watched him process it, slow, careful, a man used to vetting what he believed. Then his face relaxed.

"Thank you," he said.

She nodded. She didn't say "you're welcome" because that wasn't the tone of this conversation. She said, "Rest. Eat when you're hungry. I'll be back tomorrow."

She left him at the table and drove back to town.

That was what she did. That was what she was for.

In the spare room off the equipment bay, Owen slept deeply. His breathing was steady and slow, his body finally at rest. The pack bond, which couldn't reach a wolf who wasn't a member, offered a wordless acknowledgment that a thing was in the right place for now. Cole poured himself coffee and stood at the window, watching the eastern sky finish its work of becoming day.

～

Owen left on Monday morning.

He came to Cole before first light, in human form, with the air of a man who had made a decision and was going to carry it out without ceremony. He stood straighter than he had on Saturday. His eyes tracked without the lag they had shown.

"I'm going east," he said.

"I know." Cole had known since Saturday. Owen wasn't a man who stayed. He had been in motion long enough that stillness was only temporary now, a rest stop rather than a destination. "Is there somewhere you're heading?"

"Maybe." He said it with the uncertainty of someone who wasn't going to commit to hope. "Maybe there's a place east."

Cole looked at him. All those years of carrying this pack, of watching what happened to the ones who lost theirs. Owen wasn't in the worst state Cole had seen. He wasn't good, either. He was somewhere in the middle, which meant the coming months would make the difference.

"If you hear of anyone like you," Cole said, "who needs somewhere to stop, they can stop here."

Owen looked at him. "You'd take them in."

"We'd assess the situation. Same as we did with you."

A pause. "I'll pass it along."

He left without saying anything else, moving east through the trees in the pre-dawn dark, and Cole stood on the HQ steps and watched him go with the texture of a man who has made the right call and understands the weight it carries.

A wolf without a pack doesn't last, Old Tom had said. Which was true. Cole knew it was true because he had watched it happen. He had also watched what happened when a pack chose not to look away from a damaged wolf.

That choice carried weight too. It moved through the territory in ways that weren't visible but were real, through the knowledge that traveled between shifters, as shifters had always shared knowledge; through proximity and scent and the half-understood geography of a species that had been scattered and was always, in some incomplete way, looking for each other.

Word would reach the ones who needed to hear it. It always did. A pack that took in strays became known for that. A pack that turned them away became known for that too. The reputation traveled through channels Cole didn't fully understand, but that he had seen work, a phone call from someone who knew someone, a name passed along at a territory meeting, a lone wolf who showed up at the boundary knowing exactly where to go.

Owen was gone. The trees had swallowed him. Somewhere to the east, he would keep moving, or he would find what he was looking for, or he wouldn't find it. Cole couldn't control what happened next. He could only control what had happened here, that Blackpine had offered rest to a damaged soul.

He stood on the steps for another minute. The eastern sky was beginning to lighten at the horizon, the first gray of it, the mountains taking shape out of the dark. He had stood on these steps more times than he could count, in every season, at every hour. He knew what this sky looked like at this time of year.

He knew this now. His father had been an Alpha who was strong when strength was required, and open when openness was the harder choice. His father had made that choice a dozen times. He had watched him make it.

This morning, he had made it too.

He went inside and started the coffee. The pack would wake soon. There would be work to do. There was always work to do.

EIGHTEEN

FRANK

He arrived on Tuesday afternoon in a gray sedan she recognized from a hundred childhood pickups and drop-offs, the car her father had driven for twelve years, with a loyalty to objects that was one of his more legible qualities. She saw it from the store window before she saw him.

She didn't panic. She had been waiting for this, as you wait for an arrival you know is coming but can't schedule, alert to it, not dreading it, understanding that it had to happen and that the outcome depended on how she handled it.

Frank Thornton was fifty-three years old and had spent nineteen of those years working with the patience of a county assessor who understood that public records didn't lie; they only withheld. He wasn't a large man. He was a precise one. He had been deeply uncertain about one thing for a long time and had finally decided to go look at it himself.

He came through the door. The bell shrieked.

Their eyes met.

"Dad," she said.

"Lily." He looked around the store with the involuntary assessment of a man whose eyes cataloged spaces for anomalies. She watched him. She knew what he was seeing, a general store in a small Montana town, familiar as childhood places were, slightly smaller than memory. He was also seeing the inventory she had reorganized, the shelves in their new configuration, and the condition of a space that had been worked on with attention. He would note that, too. He noted everything.

He set the folder on the counter.

She studied it. Thick. He had been thorough.

"I told you I was going to keep the files," he said.

"You said you weren't going to look at them."

"I looked at them." He said it the way he had approached the work itself, no apology because none was owed. He was a county assessor. Looking was his function. Stopping was a promise he had made with the best of intentions and against the grain of his entire professional life. "There's more in here than what we talked about on the phone."

She glanced from the folder to her father.

He opened it.

Lily looked at the stack of papers, the photocopied documents, and the handwritten notes in her father's precise script. He had been working on this. Not casually, not as a side project. He had been working on it as he did anything that mattered to him, thoroughly, systematically, without stopping until he understood what he was looking at.

She knew the impulse. She had inherited it. The need to know, the inability to leave a question unresolved. She had spent the past weeks doing the same thing he had been doing, just with different tools and access.

THE FOLDER HELD two weeks of additional work. He had traced the land trust signatories through the county records, following each name as it passed from generation to generation of Mercers, each transfer executed with the precision of people who knew exactly what they were doing within a legal framework they had designed to be permanent. He had found the 1942 survey and gone back further, a 1901 homestead claim that used language for the parcel he hadn't seen in any other homestead claim in the county's records. He had found a reference in a 1931 county meeting transcript to "the Mercer arrangement" cited as precedent for a completely unrelated property dispute, which meant that the county's institutional memory had treated the Mercer arrangement as established fact for at least ninety years.

"This goes back before Montana was a state," he said. "The arrangement predates statehood. Whatever it is, it was set up when this was still federal territory, and it has been maintained through every legal transition since."

She listened. She let him lay it out as he needed to, in

order, with the logic of a person who had been building this case and needed to put it down somewhere.

When he finished, her attention shifted from the folder to him.

She could see what the research had cost him. Not in money or time, but in the currency of a man who had held a question for nineteen years and had finally let himself pursue it. He had broken his own promise. He had looked at the files. He had done it because he couldn't stop himself, because the data was there and he was a man who followed data. Now he stood in front of her, the consequences of that pursuit spread across the counter.

He wasn't apologizing. He was a county assessor. He didn't apologize for doing his job. But he was also her father, and she could see the other thing beneath the professional presentation, the worry, the need to understand, the protective instinct that had been running since she arrived in Blackpine.

"Dad," she said. "I know."

He paused. "You know."

"Not everything in the folder. But the shape of it. What it means and what it's for." She kept her voice even. "I found the part you haven't found yet."

His eyes narrowed. She could see him running through the implications of that sentence, the county assessor's instinct trying to identify which fact might exist that he hadn't yet found in the public record.

"What part?" he said.

"I'm not going to tell you today. When I am, I will. But what I need you to understand right now is that I looked at this as clearly as you have, and what I found didn't scare me. It made me want to stay."

He was quiet. He was the quiet of a man who had prepared for a different conversation.

"You can't ask me to accept that without knowing what you found," he said.

"I'm not asking you to accept it. I'm asking you to trust that I can assess a situation accurately." She kept her voice even and her attention on him. "I've been doing that for six years in an emergency room. I'm good at it."

His eyes stayed on hers. She held his gaze. The assessment was the same one she had been holding up to all the Blackpine scrutiny for the last weeks, the one that wanted to see what was underneath. She was the same person she had been with all of them, clear, unhurried, not performing certainty she didn't have.

"Everything changed when I got here," she said. "I wasn't expecting it to. I came for Dottie, and I came because I needed somewhere to stop. I found a reason to stay." She paused. "And I looked at it clearly and I chose it."

Frank said nothing.

"Are you happy?" he asked.

It landed like the rarest thing she could remember him saying to her, because he was a man who expressed love through function, through the Friday calls and the record research, watching over her from a precise distance for as long as she could remember. He hadn't asked her that directly, not once, in all the years since her mother left and he had rebuilt himself around the practical management of what could go wrong.

"Yes," she said.

His eyes searched her face. She could see the recalibration happening, Frank running a different kind of assessment now, one that had her face as the primary data.

He closed the folder. The sound was quiet in the empty store, the soft thump of a file that had been open for weeks being set down.

She studied her father. He seemed older than he had the last time she saw him, which had been in Bozeman, the week before she left for Blackpine. The drive had taken a toll on him. The research had taken a toll on him. The conversation they had just had, in which she had asked him to trust without verifying, had taken its own toll.

But he had closed the folder. He had set it down. That mattered.

~

SHE CALLED Jace from the back room.

"My father is here," she said. "He came to see it for himself. The conversation went well. I think you should meet him."

A pause. She knew what the pause contained, Jace's family had been the subject of nineteen years of county records research, and now he was about to meet Frank.

"Tonight?" he asked.

"Tonight would be better than him driving back to Billings with nothing but the folder."

"All right."

He came at six. Frank was still at the store, which was closed by then. The three of them sat at the table in the back where she and Jace had sat together in those first weeks. It wasn't a comfortable meeting. Frank was a county assessor who had spent considerable time and effort investigating Jace's family, and Jace was a man who understood exactly what Frank had found and what it meant that Frank had found it. The table between them held the tension of two people calculating each other.

Lily let them calculate. She had seen this before in the ER, when two specialists met over a complicated case, the mutual assessment, the careful establishment of professional territory, the feel of two people who were good at their jobs and knew it, and who were figuring out how to work together. Frank and Jace weren't specialists. But they were operating in the same mode, each trying to understand what the other was and what that meant.

She stayed quiet. She let it happen. She had learned in the ER that some processes couldn't be rushed, and the process of two careful men learning to trust each other was one of them.

Over the course of an hour, she watched what happened when Frank Thornton encountered a person who didn't perform. Jace was open. He was always open. It wasn't performance; it was who he was. But he was also direct in a way Frank understood, as he recognized people who operated on facts rather than impressions. He answered Frank's questions without embellishment. He didn't offer information he hadn't been asked for. He didn't rush the meeting.

Frank asked about the property records. Jace confirmed what Frank had found without elaborating on what Frank hadn't.

Frank asked about the rescue operation. Jace told him what BWR did, accurately.

Frank asked about Lily.

Jace paused before answering. She watched him consider the question, consider the man asking it, and consider what kind of answer Frank Thornton needed to hear versus what kind of answer would make the situation easier. She knew what he would choose. He always chose the harder version when the harder version was more true.

"She makes her own decisions," he said. "She made this one. I'm glad she did. But she made it."

Frank studied him for a long time. He was assessing Jace, doing his own kind of calculating.

He didn't warm. He wasn't that kind of man. But the nature of the tension changed. It became the tension of two people who had understood each other rather than the tension of two people who hadn't yet assessed each other.

Frank drove back to Billings the next morning. He had declined the offer of Dottie's spare room, as Lily had expected. He needed to go back to his space and sit with this. He was a person who processed through solitude, record-keeping, and the discipline of a man who had learned that his feelings were safest when they had somewhere to go.

She had made him breakfast. He had eaten it without conversation, the quiet of a man who had said what he was going to say the night before and was now in the mode of observation and digestion. She knew this about her father. She had grown up with it. The silences weren't empty; they were full of processing.

At the door, he had paused. He had looked at her as he had when she was eleven years old and her mother had left, and he had been trying to figure out how to be a single parent to a daughter he didn't fully understand. The same expression, twenty years later. The same uncertainty underneath the competence.

"I'll call on Friday," he said. "The regular call."

"I'll be there," she said.

He drove away.

She stood for a while in the cold November morning, looking at the empty street and the mountains beyond it, white and sharp above the town. The town was quiet at this hour. A light was on at the Summit Diner, the shape of Marge's silhouette behind the counter, starting the coffee. A truck was going north on the main road. The stillness of a small town in November, before anyone was moving, when the day was still just potential. The bell above the door would ring in an hour, when she opened for the day. Earl would come down from upstairs. Dottie, who had known Frank was here and had given them space as she gave things the space they needed, would appear at the kitchen table for tea, look at Lily with the eyes that saw all of it, and say nothing until Lily was ready.

She hadn't given Frank the full picture. She had given him what he could absorb, which was what you did with the people you loved who processed differently than you. He was a county assessor. He would go back to Billings, open the folder on his desk, look at it with the new information she had given him, run it against what he had found, and find that it held. She knew this about her father; he believed what the evidence supported, and she was the evidence.

He had closed the folder. That was what she had needed him to do.

The rest could come when it was ready.

She went inside. Dottie was at the kitchen table with her tea, looking at her with the eyes that had been watching this family for thirty years.

"He's a good man," Dottie said. "He's always been a good man. He just doesn't know how to show it."

"I know."

"Give him time. He'll figure it out." Dottie took a sip of her tea. "Your grandfather was the same way, early on. Took him fifteen years to learn how to say what he meant instead of what he thought he should say."

"Fifteen years."

"Well." The corner of Dottie's mouth moved. "Frank's had a head start. He's been practicing on you for thirty-two."

Lily laughed. It was the first laugh she had had since

Frank arrived, and it came out of her cleanly, like a release that had been waiting for permission.

She sat across from her grandmother, took a cup of tea, and let the morning settle around her. The folder was on the counter. She would deal with it later. Right now, there was tea, and Dottie, and the quiet of a store that had been in her family for decades.

She sat there, letting the morning settle around her, and didn't try to make it more than it was. The rest would come. It always did, in Blackpine, slowly, in the right order, at the pace of a place that had been doing things its own way longer than any of them had been alive. She was learning to trust that pace. It wasn't a small lesson.

CHAPTER

NINETEEN

THE THRESHOLD

Pack dinner on Friday was the same as it had always been, except that Lily was at the table.

Not as she had been at the table, as a guest pulled in by Nora's hospitality and still finding the room's edges. She was at the table as Harper was at the table; she occupied her chair with ease, understanding she was supposed to be here. She knew where the water glasses were. She knew that Danny's relationship with the serving spoon was idiosyncratic, that Reid took the end seat, that Eli always arrived slightly late and always acted like he hadn't, and that Old Tom's stories arrived in the third act of dinner, when the food was gone and the pace of conversation had moved to the unhurried kind.

She had been here eight weeks, and she knew the table better than some people knew tables they had sat at for years.

Jace remembered the first time Harper had come to a pack dinner, eight months ago, still finding the shape of

201

the table, the order of things, how the room worked. Harper had figured it out. She had figured it out the same way Lily had, by paying attention, by being present, by doing the work of belonging without asking anyone to make it easier for her.

Lily was different from Harper in most ways. She was quieter, more watchful, more inclined to file information than to act on it immediately. But in this one way, she was exactly the same; she understood that belonging was earned, not granted, and she had earned it.

Jace watched her talk to Nora about the supply order she had been building, the medical items she was sourcing through her professional supplier account, in a way that wouldn't trace back to Blackpine. He watched Harper lean across the table to contribute, and Lily write a note on the edge of her napkin, as she did everywhere, in the margin of whatever was nearest. He watched Cole watch Lily with the Alpha's satisfaction of a man who had been missing a piece of the pack's capability for a long time and had found it.

His wolf was doing the thing it did at pack dinners now, which was the settled, easy nature of a thing in its element. He had been coming to these dinners for twelve years. The pack had grown and changed over that time, as packs did. He had watched his brother find Harper and watched Harper become the person who sat at the table and ran the pack's public narrative with the same ease that Cole ran its operations. He had wondered, in the years between, if it would always be just the two of them at the top, himself and Cole, carrying it without the ballast of a person who belonged to you.

He wasn't wondering anymore.

After dinner, when the table was being cleared and Old Tom had told the bear story and Danny had gotten into a detailed technical discussion with Reid that no one else fully understood, Jace caught Lily's eye.

She read the question in his face. She set down the plates she was holding and handed them to Nora without explanation, and Nora took them with the absence of comment that meant she saw it all and intended to say nothing.

They got their coats and went out.

THE TERRITORY at night in November was beautiful in a particular way; the cold was sharp enough to be present without being punishing, the sky clear, the snow on the ground catching the ambient light and turning it back into soft illumination. He had run this territory his whole life. He had run it in wolf form and in human form, in every weather the mountains made. He knew it as he knew the table, without having to think about it.

He had told her about the clearing in October, in the store, over coffee. Past the western property line, where the pack's land meets the national forest. He had said *you should come sometime*, and she had said *I'd like that*, and neither of them had pushed on the when because there were things that needed to happen first.

Those steps had happened.

She walked beside him without asking where they were going. She had enough of the territory in her now, from the access road, the boundary trail, and the BWR approach, to orient herself roughly by the tree line and the mountain shape. She knew they were heading west. She knew what was west.

The cold was serious. He was indifferent to it in a way she wasn't. He pulled off his jacket without ceremony and held it out to her.

"I have a coat," she said.

"Your coat is handling November. My jacket is an additional layer."

She took it and put it on over her coat, which made her look slightly comical and bundled, and she looked at him with the expression that wasn't quite a smile and was better than one.

They walked.

THE CLEARING OPENED up as he had described it, above the tree line, the sky wider than in the forest below, the northern range laid out across the horizon in the arrangement of peaks he had been looking at his whole life. The snow was deeper up here, undisturbed except for animal tracks at the edges. It was a place with a character of its own, separate from the pack business, the boundary logistics, and the maps with their annotations. His father had brought him here because it was the place where the territory stopped being work and became sacred ground.

He stopped at the center of the clearing.

Lily stood beside him, looking at the mountains.

He had planned, at various points over the past two months, how this moment would go. He had drafted versions of it in his head as he drafted his words when the stakes were high enough, methodically, considering the sequencing, thinking about what needed to be said first. He had been anticipating this conversation since October.

What he found, standing in the clearing with the mountains in front of them, the cold air in his lungs, and Lily's breath visible in the night air, was that the versions he had drafted were the wrong shape for the actual thing.

"I need to tell you," he said.

She turned to look at him. She waited.

"I've known since the first day," he said. "What you were to me. The bond knows before you do. That's how it works, and I explained the biology of that to you in the cabin. You know the mechanics." He looked at her. "What I haven't said is the other part. Which is that I would have chosen this anyway."

She was watching him intently, giving him her full attention.

"The bond told me what you were. It didn't make the choice for me. I made the choice. I made it every time I drove past the store and then drove back. I made it when I started coming in, when I said I owed you an explanation, and when I called you from a forest floor at ten o'clock on a Friday night because you were who I wanted to call." He fixed his eyes on her. "I choose this. I choose you. Not because the bond says so, but because the bond just told me first. I'm saying it because I mean it and because you should know the difference."

The mountains held their silence.

Lily looked at him for a long time. He watched her process it with the quality she had when words landed at depth rather than on the surface, the nurse's careful distinction between what you were told and what you understood.

"I know the difference," she said. "I've known it for a while."

He nodded.

"I want to tell you as well," she said.

"All right."

She looked at the clearing. At the shape of the space, the tree line on three sides, the mountains open to the north, the undisturbed snow. "This is where I want it to happen," she said. "The claiming. Not the cabin, not the HQ. Here."

He hadn't anticipated that. The claiming had always been abstract in his planning. A when and a how but not a where, because the where hadn't presented itself. She had looked at the clearing for thirty seconds and found the where.

"Here," he said.

"Yes." She shifted so she was fully toward him. "When it's time. I'm not in a hurry. I want to understand it fully first and I want it to be right, which is what you wanted for this. I learned that from you." She paused. "I want it to be the place your father brought you."

He looked at her. The moonlight caught the clarity of her expression, the steadiness that wasn't performance but who she was. She had thought about this. She had chosen the location the way she chose everything, carefully, with full information, and with an understanding of what it would mean.

He didn't say anything.

His father had brought him here the summer he was nine and had spoken words about the territory that Jace had carried for twenty-two years without always knowing he was carrying them. *This is where you understand what it means to belong to a purpose larger than yourself.* It had been about the pack, about the territory, about the burden of what the Mercer family was in Blackpine. He had carried it forward because it was true, because every time he came to this clearing he felt it again.

He hadn't thought about sharing it. Not the clearing itself. He had offered that in October in the store over coffee. But the weight behind it.

"Okay," he said.

The word was inadequate to what he felt, a feeling larger than language, an emotion that lived in the space where the wolf and the man were the same. She had chosen the place where his father had brought him. She had chosen it not because he had explained it to her, but because she had been paying attention for eight weeks and had learned the shape of the things that mattered to him.

This was what it meant to be seen. This was what it meant to be chosen by someone who chose with full information.

They stood in the clearing in the cold for a while, with the mountains to the north, the snow around them, and a decision that had been made without anyone saying it was a decision.

WALKING BACK, she thought about the shape of the last eight weeks.

She had arrived in October not knowing what she was heading toward. She had done what she always did, observed, filed, and waited for the picture to clarify. She hadn't expected the picture to be this. She hadn't expected any of it, not the way the town fitted itself around her, not the way the pack had a space in it that had been waiting for her skills, not the way a man she had known at the edges of her summers had turned out to be the person she had been adjacent to her whole life without understanding what the adjacency meant.

She had understood it now.

The cold was serious and he ran hot enough that standing near him was a different temperature than standing in the dark alone. The heat of him was the heat of a wolf, and it was also the solidity of this person who had chosen her, in the clearing of a mountain territory at night, in the vocabulary of a man who had learned to be careful and had decided to stop.

She had chosen him too.

This was the fact she had been arriving at since October, not the biology, not the bond mechanics, not the land trust or the century-old arrangement or the pack's formal welcome. Those were the context. The choice was hers. She had looked at all of it and she had chosen with the clarity she'd spent years building, the choice that was true versus the choice that was merely compelling.

It was true.

She had his jacket around her shoulders, which still smelled of the forest and the clean cold of November at altitude. She would give it back when they reached the HQ parking area. She was going to drive back to town. She was going to open the store tomorrow and the day after, and she was going to build the practice that didn't yet exist and learn the medicine of treating bodies that healed in ways the textbooks hadn't covered.

She was going to stay.

She had been saying this for two weeks, to Cole and to Frank and to Earl with his kettle and to Dottie with her thirty years of patient waiting. She had been saying it and it had been true and it was becoming more true the way that some things became more true over time rather than less, the way a diagnosis became more certain as the data accumulated.

The HQ lights were visible through the trees.

She glanced at him. He was watching her with the expression she had been cataloging for eight weeks, the one she now had a complete picture of. The steadiness and the weight behind it, the full measure of it, nothing managed.

"The clearing," she said.

"The clearing," he confirmed.

They walked the rest of the way to the parking area in silence, but it wasn't the silence of things unsaid. It was the silence of things that had been said and understood and that didn't need to be repeated. The territory held them. The cold held them. The weight of what they had decided held them both.

At her car, she handed back his jacket. He took it without ceremony. She opened the door, then paused and looked at him.

"I'm glad I came back," she said.

He knew what she meant. Not just tonight. Not just the clearing. All of it, October, the store, the truth, the pack, the choice. She was glad she had come back to Blackpine. She was glad she had stayed.

"So am I," he said.

She got in the car. He watched her drive away, the taillights disappearing down the access road, and then he stood in the cold for another minute, looking at the trees and the mountains and the shape of a life that had just gotten larger.

The clearing. When it was time. He would wait as long as she needed. He had already waited years for a person he hadn't known he was waiting for. He could wait a little longer now that he knew.

The cold was clean and sharp. The stars were bright. The territory was quiet around him, the pack bond humming its low steady frequency in the back of his awareness. Everything was exactly where it was supposed to be.

He stood there a moment longer, then turned and went inside. The HQ was quiet, the pack bond humming at its low frequency, the building doing what it did at this hour, holding the territory's edge. He stood in it for a minute, then turned off the lights and drove home, and his wolf had nothing left to be restless about.

CHAPTER

TWENTY

THE HOT SPRING

He arrived at the store on Saturday morning with the contained quality he had when he intended to show her a place, steady, satisfied, not requiring her to be impressed before she had seen it.

She was behind the counter with the weekly accounts. Her attention lifted when the bell shrieked.

"Get your coat," he said.

She studied him, then the accounts, which were half done. She put down the pen.

EARL CALLED from the back room, "I've got it."

This was a pattern she had noticed about Earl in the past two weeks. He had developed a habit of appearing at precisely the moment his presence would remove an obstacle to Lily leaving the store. She hadn't confirmed that this was coordinated. She was also not going to confirm that it wasn't.

She got her coat.

He drove west on the mountain road past the BWR access lane, onto a track she hadn't taken before, narrower, winding through the pines like a road that had been made by use rather than intention. The truck moved through it with the ease of a vehicle that had made this passage many times.

"Where are we going?" she asked.

"You'll know it when you see it."

She looked out the window at the pine trees. The mountain light at this hour was the one she knew now, low from the south, the brief gold it made in the snow between the trees before it faded. Nine weeks. She knew the shapes of the territory the way she knew the shapes of the store's rhythms, not by map but by accumulation, by the memory of a body that had moved through a place enough times to stop needing to think about where it was going.

She didn't know this road.

He parked at the end of it, where the pines opened onto a rock shelf, and they got out.

The smell reached her before anything else. The mineral note of thermal water, the faint sulfur beneath it that wasn't unpleasant, a combination that her nurse's brain catalogued as *geothermal source, significant mineral content, benign.* The steam was visible above the rock, rising in thin columns into the cold air, moving as steam moved in the November stillness when the air was cold enough to hold it briefly before it dissolved.

She walked to the edge of the shelf.

Below it, in the bowl of rock, the spring. A natural pool, the size of a large room, its edges defined by the rock shelf on three sides and the creek bank on the fourth. The water was clear enough to see the bottom, the mineral deposits giving it a blue-green quality, not artificial, the color of geology rather than treatment. The steam came off it in slow continuous plumes. Around the edges, where the thermal kept the water heated against the air, the frost that had accumulated on the surrounding rock stopped in a clean line.

She assessed it as she assessed everything, temperature differential significant, steam density suggesting surface temperature well above ambient, no visible discoloration indicating hazardous mineral content, pool size adequate, edges accessible.

Then the second thing happened, which was that she stopped cataloging.

There was a quality to this place that had nothing to do with its temperature. She had been in Blackpine long enough now to recognize when a place held history, the accumulated presence of a location that had been used by the same people in the same ways for a long time, the way it held that use until it became part of what the place was. The general store had it. The HQ had it. This had it in a different key, older and quieter, the quality that came from decades of the pack returning to the same place and leaving a piece of themselves in the ground.

She studied it for a long time.

"The pack hot spring," she said. It wasn't a question.

"Harper saw it once, from a distance," he said. "Cole hadn't invited her in yet." He stood beside her looking at the pool with the ease of someone looking at a familiar sight. "My father used to bring the pack here after the full runs. Late fall, when the temperature dropped enough to make the contrast matter." He paused. "It's ours. The family's, the pack's. It's been here as long as the territory has."

She scanned the steam, and the clear water and the rock shelf, and the way the mountains were visible above the tree line to the north, the same arrangement of peaks she knew by now.

"All right," she said.

THE WATER WAS hotter than she had expected, hot enough to be serious about, a characteristic of heat that wasn't the heat of a bath or a pool but the heat of geology, warmth that came from the earth's own temperature rather than from an external source. It had density to it. She felt it settle against her skin and understood what he had meant about the contrast, outside, the air was thirty degrees; in the water, she was in a different season entirely.

She had her back to the rock shelf. He was across the pool, which wasn't far. The steam was thin at the surface, moving slowly. The pines above them held their November stillness.

She had a professional's relationship with her body's responses, readable, not felt. She was aware of the heat-against-heat characteristic of being in the water near a person whose baseline temperature ran several degrees above a human's, the physics of two heat sources in the same medium. She was aware that this was the first time they had been this close without urgency or crisis providing the frame. She was aware of what that meant.

He was watching her with the expression she had spent two months learning. In the steam and the low light it had its full quality; the steadiness and the weight behind it, and the bearing of a man who had spent years behind a wall and had chosen to come out from behind it.

She moved through the water toward him.

Not far. The pool wasn't large. She was close enough to feel his body heat, as she had before. And now she knew what to do.

She put her hand on his shoulder as she had put her hand on his shoulder in wolf form on a cold November morning three weeks ago, with the clarity of a person who has arrived at a thing and is choosing it. He held still. He let her arrive.

"I've been looking at you," she said, "since the first day you walked through that door."

"I know," he said. "I've known."

The steam moved between them and over them. The mountains were there above the tree line, white and clear.

He brought his hand up to the side of her face, his palm fever-hot against her cheek, and their eyes locked.

He kissed her.

Not the way the first kiss had been, the morning after the cabin. This was different. This was the kiss of two people who knew each other, who had made their choices and were done pretending a kiss could contain it all. His hand slid from her face to her waist, then lower, steady even in the water, giving her time to stop him. She didn't. She moved closer until there was no water between their bodies.

He kissed her again, slower this time, his mouth taking its time with hers until her whole body tightened around the waiting. She felt the roughness of his palm at her back, the strong line of his chest against her breasts, the unmistakable shape of his arousal against her thigh. The knowledge of it went through her in a direct, clean line. No abstraction. No theory. Just want.

"Lily," he said against her mouth. "Tell me if you want me to stop."

Her eyes held his. Steam curled around them, thin and white in the cold air, and the mountains stood above the tree line as if they had all the time in the world. "I don't," she said. "I want more."

The words changed him. Not into someone else. Into more fully himself. He lifted her onto the shallow rock shelf at the pool's edge, where the water covered her hips and thighs, and knelt between her knees with the focus he brought to what mattered. He kissed her throat, then the upper curve of one breast, where it rose wet above the water, his hands opening over her waist as if he were learning the shape by touch rather than by memory.

She made a sound she had never made in a clinical setting and never would. His hand slipped between her thighs with a patient certainty that made her grip the slick rock behind her. Nothing about it was hurried. He watched her face as he touched her, adjusted to her, and learned what made her breath catch and what made her arch toward him. The steam, the cold air, and the water all disappeared beneath the simple fact of what he was doing to her.

"Jace." His name came out broken and honest.

"I know." His voice was low, close, meant only for her. He touched her until the pressure inside her crested and broke, hard enough that her back arched and her hands fisted against the stone. He stayed with her through it, steady as it moved through her in wave after wave, his mouth at her breast, his eyes on hers when she could focus again.

She was still shaking when he rose and kissed her. She tasted herself on his mouth and answered him, both hands on his shoulders, pulling him in because she wasn't interested in caution anymore. "I want all of you," she said.

He held her face for a second, searching for hesitation and finding none. Then he entered her in one slow, deliberate push that made her head fall back against the rock. The water shifted around them. He stopped there, breathing hard, giving her space to choose again.

She tightened her legs around him and drew him deeper. "Don't stop."

He didn't. He moved with the same deliberate control he brought to the rest of his life until control gave way to hunger and the rhythm between them turned urgent, water slipping against their skin, the cold air sharp at her shoulders while the rest was sensation and pressure and the deep rightness of finally having this. She could feel the exact point where restraint left him. She met it with her own.

When she reached her climax again, it took her by surprise, stronger than the first, a hard, bright release that pulled his name from her. He followed with a rough sound she felt more than heard, then kissed her once, deeply, like a promise finished rather than begun.

They stayed like that for a minute, water moving around them, both breathing hard. Then he eased back and pulled her into him, her cheek against his shoulder, his hand heavy and possessive at the base of her spine. The steam rose. The territory held. This time there was no question about what kind of place this was for them.

She had never claimed to be a good cook.

This wasn't modesty. It was accurate, years in emergency medicine, twelve-hour shifts that ended with takeout or cereal, and a habit of cooking that had never had the right conditions to develop. She knew how to make coffee. She knew how to make the scrambled eggs she had been making since she was fourteen. She knew pasta as every person who had ever lived alone for an extended period knew pasta, well enough not to ruin it but not well enough to do anything interesting with it.

His kitchen, however, was the kitchen of a man who knew what he was doing. He had cast iron. He had dried herbs in labeled jars. He had a cutting board that was clearly older than most of her furniture and bore the patina of a tool used regularly with care.

She found the pasta.

"You don't have to," he said. He was at the kitchen table with a cup of coffee, watching her navigate the space without comment.

"I know I don't have to." She found the olive oil. "I want to."

"There's garlic in the drawer to the left of the stove."

"I see it."

He drank his coffee. She moved through his kitchen with the efficiency she brought to work, and the uncertainty of someone operating in unfamiliar territory, which wasn't a combination she was accustomed to. In the ER, she had always known the layout. Here she was learning it in real time, reaching for things in the wrong place and then correcting, finding the rhythm of this kitchen, the way the burners ran hot and the drawer stuck, and the colander was above the stove rather than below it.

She made pasta with garlic and olive oil. It wasn't, she thought, her best work. The garlic had gone slightly past golden before she caught it. He ate it without comment, except that he ate it all, which she noted as meaningful data.

After dinner, she found she still didn't want to leave.

She had been here before—the kitchen where she had stayed until three in the morning learning what he was, the couch where she had slept in her coat, the table where they had sat with coffee in the quiet of a cabin at altitude in November. She knew where the mugs were. She knew the sound the stove made when it was running correctly. The pull of this place had the feel of a destination she had been heading toward for a long time without knowing the address.

She stayed, and when he touched her again in the quiet of the cabin, there was no hesitation left in either of them.

He added a log to the stove, and she sat on the couch with her coffee, watching him do it with the ease of someone entirely at home in a space, no performance, no negotiation of presence. This was what domesticity looked like for him. She had been cataloging this about him, how he occupied space without waste, without display, without the constant negotiation of presence that most people engaged in.

She had chosen well. She allowed herself to think this plainly, without qualification.

Outside, the November dark had settled in with the altitude, the darkness of no ambient light, the stars beginning to show through the cabin window above the tree line. The fire in the stove ticked. The coffee was good.

"The garlic," she said.

"What about it?"

"I caught it too late."

His expression held what might have been amusement. "It was fine."

"It was almost burned."

"Almost burned is different from burned." He drank his coffee. "You'll get it."

She raised an eyebrow. "You're going to let me cook in your kitchen again."

"I'm going to let you cook in this kitchen as many times as you want." He said it, as he said things that were statements of fact, and also everything else.

She drank her coffee and let the evening settle around them as evenings were settling around her in Blackpine now, a place that had become hers, a man who was hers, and nothing urgent anywhere.

SUNDAY MORNING, she went to the Summit Diner properly.

Not the quick coffee she had grabbed twice in October, standing at the counter with her coat on because she was only stopping for a minute. This time she sat at a table, took off her coat, and looked at the menu with the attention it deserved. There was significance in the act of sitting down in a place, of taking off your coat, that announced a different kind of presence. She had been doing this in Blackpine for nine weeks, arriving, and then arriving differently, each arrival a deeper version of the same choice. The Summit Diner had been part of the furniture of her Blackpine since childhood, the smell of it, the comfort it offered even in winter, the way Marge ran the floor. Forty years in, and she hadn't slowed.

Marge came to the table.

She assessed Lily with eyes that took in a room in a single sweep and had clearly taken in everything about Lily Thornton, her presence in Blackpine, and how she looked this Sunday morning, and had reached a conclusion.

"Huckleberry pie," she said. She didn't ask.

"I was going to start with coffee."

"You can have both." Marge wrote nothing on her pad. She would remember. She always remembered. "He told you to come," she said. It wasn't a question either.

"He said it was the best part of Blackpine."

Marge's mouth moved as it had when she found a statement both amusing and accurate. "He's been saying that since October," she said. "I didn't think he meant the pie."

She went to get the coffee.

Lily sat at the table in the Summit Diner, looking out the window at the Sunday morning street, the mountains visible above the roofline, and what it meant to have a Blackpine Sunday in late November, quiet and deliberate, the town doing its weekend thing without apology. Mrs. Patterson going past with her supplement bag. A truck she recognized as Danny's idling at the hardware store. The water tower at the edge of town. All of it familiar now.

The pie arrived.

It was, she was prepared to acknowledge, the best pie in Blackpine.

She ate it slowly. Outside, Blackpine went about its Sunday business. The mountains stayed where they were. She had been here two months, which wasn't long by the town's standard of measurement, and she was learning to measure time the way the town did, not by the clock but by the accumulation of small details. The way Marge remembered her order. The fact that she now knew which truck was Danny's. These were the markers that meant you were staying, even before you said so.

TWENTY-ONE

THE RUN

R eid collected the soil sample Monday morning.

He had been waiting for a window since Saturday, when Owen arrived and the pack bond pulled the whole team into a different problem. The window was Monday, with Owen gone, the northern corridor quiet in the way that follows disruption, the way of a territory that has processed the disruption and returned to its own rhythm. Reid went out before dawn with a sampling kit and the methodical patience of a man who understood that the soil would tell him exactly what it had been holding for as long as it had been holding it, and that patience was the appropriate response.

He brought the sample back to HQ at seven. He put it on the table where Lily would find it, with a single handwritten note.

mile four, east side, depth three inches, six-inch radius. —R.

This was Reid's version of a summary report.

Jace called Lily when he knew she would be at the store. "The sample's here," he said. "Reid got it this morning."

A brief pause. He could hear her processing, the nurse's inventory, adding this to the open file she had been keeping. "I'll come by Tuesday," she said. "I want to run some tests first."

He understood what she meant by tests. Not the lab tests that required equipment she didn't have. The nurse's field assessment, a set of preliminary checks that wouldn't identify the compound but might narrow the category. She had been building the protocol since he told her about the sample some weeks ago. It was already in her notebook.

"Tuesday," he confirmed.

He put the phone down and went to find Cole.

Cole was at the map table, where he usually was. He was looking at the northern corridor, where his attention usually was this month. His eyes lifted when Jace came in.

"Reid got the sample."

Cole nodded. He turned back to the map. His finger moved over the eastern edge, the miles-three-to-six stretch, the space where the traps had been and the blinds and the chemical deposit, all of it in the same corridor, all of it with the same patience behind it.

"Tonight," Cole said. "Weather's right."

He meant the run. Jace had known. The pack ran when the conditions were right and when the pack needed it, and after two weeks of tension, the tension hadn't resolved but had settled into the watchfulness of a pack that understood its territory and was operating accordingly. A run wasn't an answer to what was happening in the northern corridor. It was a way of being the thing you were, moving through your territory in full form, the pack bond running at its full capacity, the land under your feet, and the cold air and the mountains above.

"Tonight," Jace agreed.

He thought about Lily on the hot spring's edge two days before, looking at the pool with a clinical assessment, then the second awareness beneath it, the recognition that a place could hold meaning. He thought about her in his kitchen, navigating the space with confidence, not entirely sure where items were, but going to figure it out. He thought about how the evening had settled.

He had been thinking about this, and while he was thinking about it he had been thinking about tonight.

"I want to tell Lily," he said.

Cole looked at him. "About the run."

"That we're doing it tonight. That she can come to the clearing above the tree line if she wants to." He said it as he made statements that were decided. "I'm not asking her to stay away. She's pack now. She should see this."

Cole looked at him. He was reading Jace as Alphas read their Betas, not the surface, but the actual read. He found what he was looking for.

"Tell her," he said.

THE CALL CAME in at nine.

Two trail runners from Whitefish were on a national forest route north of the pack boundary. They had filed a plan with their hotel, back by eight, filed route. It was nine, and the hotel was calling. Cole picked up his phone.

"Reid. Danny. Northeast boundary, trail five. Two runners, overdue. Take the truck and go human."

Jace looked at him.

"Go human," Cole repeated. It was November. The forest road to trail five was accessible. There was no reason to send wolves when a truck and two people with headlamps and the search-and-rescue competency the pack had been building for twelve years would do the job.

Reid and Danny were out the door in four minutes.

Jace called Lily. Not because he had to. Because she was the pack medic and because he had learned, in the nine weeks of watching her, that she preferred to be present rather than informed after the fact.

She arrived at HQ at twenty past nine.

The two trail runners came in at ten-fifteen. They had been less than a quarter mile off their intended route when Reid found them, sitting under a rock overhang where they had had the sense to stop moving when they realized they were turned around. Cold, dehydrated, mildly hypothermic by the look of them, but nothing that required more than what Lily had in the supply closet and forty minutes of methodical reheating.

She worked through both of them with the focused

attention he had watched her bring to everything medical, to Sarah's fever, to Owen's elevated temperature, to his leg in the dark. She didn't perform competence. She had it, and it showed as skills showed when they were actual rather than constructed.

He watched Cole watch Lily. The Alpha's read on a pack member doing exactly what the pack needed done. The satisfaction of a man who had been running a rescue operation for over a decade with a gap in it that had just been filled.

They loaded the runners into Danny's truck at eleven for the drive to Whitefish, which was standard protocol, stable, not emergency, hospital for observation, BWR files the call correctly. Clean.

"Good," Cole said after they had gone. He said it as he said words that were evaluations, without ceremony.

Lily was cleaning up the supply area. She didn't look up. "The short hiker tape is in the wrong section," she said. "I'm reorganizing the closet when I'm back Tuesday."

Cole looked at Jace. Jace didn't smile.

JACE TOLD her about the run at noon, after the runners had left and the HQ was quiet again. He sat across from her at the long table with coffee and said it plainly, the pack ran in full form once or twice a month, weather permitting. Tonight was a run night. If she wanted to come to the clearing above the western tree line to watch, she could.

She had been waiting for this offer since October.

"What does it look like?" she said. Not can I or should I. Just the practical question.

"It looks like what it is," he said. "All of us in wolf form, running the territory. An hour, maybe more." He held the coffee. "It's not a performance. You'd be watching us do what we do. Which is different from a demonstration."

"I know the difference," she said. "I watched you with the wolf on the access road in October. You didn't know I was there."

He looked at her.

"That's what I mean by not a performance," she said. "I've seen you shift when you thought you were alone. I know what to look for."

He nodded. "Seven. It'll be dark. Dress for it."

She had been dressing for Montana's cold for nine weeks. She dressed for it.

THE CLEARING at the edge of the western tree line was the same clearing they had walked to two weeks ago, the night of the declaration, the night she had chosen the place. It looked different at seven on a Monday in November—the sky was fully dark, the snow on the ground picking up the ambient light and turning it into soft illumination, the mountains a presence against the sky rather than a view. She stood at the clearing's edge the way she had stood at the hot spring's edge two days before, with her assessment open and her clinical vocabulary quietly falling short.

Below the clearing, the territory dropped into the darker line of the forest. She waited.

They came.

Not in a line. Not in any formation she had an analogy for. They moved through the pines below her like creatures entirely in their element, a motion unlike anything she had reference points for. She had seen Jace in wolf form twice, once in crisis on the forest floor, once in the morning light at the cabin, deliberate and still. This was neither. This was the wolf in full motion, unhesitating, and it wasn't alone.

She found him first because she knew him. The golden amber of him was visible even in the low light, the cream at his chest and throat catching the snow's ambient reflection. He moved as he moved through her grandfather's store when the store was his, with complete ease, without waste, as though the terrain were a map he had memorized and no longer needed to think about.

Cole: dark gray-blue, larger even than Jace, moving at the head of the loose grouping with the quality she had seen in Cole Mercer in human form and now understood wasn't a personality trait but a biological one. The Alpha presence. The one the pack moved in relation to.

Reid: steel-blue-gray at the far edge, moving with the precision of a tracker, the pack's point in the eastern direction, watching everything.

The others. Eli first, smaller than the rest, faster for it, cutting through the gaps in the tree line with the particular ease of a wolf built for tight terrain. Sarah. Danny. The solid presence of Old Tom's wolf form at the back of the grouping. Nora. The pack is full.

She had grown up adjacent to this. She had spent nine weeks knowing what it was without ever seeing it whole. She had the picture now, and she was looking at it. The picture wasn't what she had expected, not because she had expected fear, but because she had expected a challenge she would need to hold steady against. She had prepared herself for the clinical assessment, for the discipline of a person who was going to look at a reality that tested the edges of their framework.

It didn't test the edges. It fit.

This was what Blackpine was. This was what the mountains held, what the territory held, what the Thornton family had been adjacent to for three generations without ever being handed the full picture until now. She was looking at the full picture, and it wasn't alarming and it wasn't requiring anything from her except what she had been doing for nine weeks, which was paying attention.

The pack looped back through the lower clearing and came up toward the western tree line. She didn't move. She stayed where she was and let them come.

Jace slowed as he came through the tree line. He saw her. He held her gaze for one beat, two, with the gold eyes she knew now from both sides of what he was, the same eyes in both forms, and then the pack carried him past and she watched them go.

She stayed until they came back around.

When it was done, she went to the edge of the tree line and waited. He came to her out of the dark, in human form, pulling on his jacket. His eyes met hers with the look she now had a complete picture of.

"Well?" he asked.

"I've been looking at the wrong angle," she said. "All this time, trying to find the frame that would make it make sense. There isn't a frame. It's just what it is." Her gaze followed the dark tree line where the pack had gone. "They're beautiful."

He stood beside her. Not touching. Just there, in the ease she had come to know as his baseline.

"Yes," he said.

They walked back to the HQ through the cold.

INSIDE, Danny sat at the table with coffee and a look of elaborate casualness. Subtlety was professionally challenging for him, and it showed. He watched them come in together and couldn't keep the look off his face.

Cole, from the kitchen doorway, gave him a single look.

Danny's expression shifted to sudden, focused interest in his coffee cup.

Her eyes found Jace. His met hers. A glint in his face that might have been amusement, contained.

She went to get coffee.

Tuesday evening, she drove to his cabin after the store closed.

She had come with intention, different from the other times she had come, the morning of the shift, the night she had driven in the dark to a forest floor, the evening they had talked for three hours about what she had been standing beside her whole life. Those had been arrivals of necessity or revelation. This was neither.

She had simply wanted to be here. She was here.

He answered the door with the ease of a man who had been expecting her, which he had been, because she had texted him and he had said come over. This was also different, the ease of a rhythm that was becoming a pattern, the comfort of a routine you had done enough times to stop thinking about the mechanics of it.

She came in. He took her coat.

Later, she would reflect on the nature of their first time together, thinking of it as one does with experiences that develop over time. The intentions from both sides carried great importance. The heat of him, the elevated temperature she had logged as biological data, now the presence of the person who was with her, nothing more than that. The patience he brought to this, and what that patience looked like here, where it had nowhere to be except present. Her own steadiness, which wasn't clinical now but was hers now, the thing underneath the nurse that she didn't always let people see and that he had already seen, weeks ago on a forest floor when she had looked at a truth her vocabulary didn't cover and hadn't run.

She didn't run. She hadn't run. She wasn't going to run.

She stayed the night.

In the morning, she stirred awake to a sense of belonging that enveloped her, the warmth of the blankets cocooning her, the gentle glow of sunlight filtering through the cabin windows, and the distinct crackle of the stove signaling it was time for more firewood. She had been in this cabin enough times now to know the morning version of it. She was learning the versions of things, the store at opening, at noon, at closing. The HQ in the middle of a call and in the settled quiet after. Him in his kitchen, in the clearing, in wolf form in the cold morning light.

This version. She was learning this version too.

He was already up. She could hear him in the kitchen, the sounds of the coffeemaker and the quiet way he moved in a space he knew well. She could smell coffee. She lay in his bed in his cabin in the mountains and looked at the ceiling and thought about the shape of a life that was assembling itself around her without requiring her to force it, and was satisfied. It wasn't a simple feeling. It was the nurse's feeling, when the diagnosis is confirmed, a different aspect of patience from most people, not waiting to speak, but having already said the truth and allowing the other person to arrive at it. It isn't the bad one.

TWENTY-TWO

WHAT'S OURS

S he brought her analysis on Thursday.

Not a report. A notebook, opened to the page where she had been working the problem since Tuesday, her handwriting in the margin-dense style she used for the observations she kept, observations that weren't yet conclusions but were more than data, living in the space between what she could prove and what she understood.

He read it while she sat across the map table, waiting with the patience she had. A different form of patience from most people, not waiting to speak, but having already said the truth and allowing the other person to arrive at it.

Not natural. Not accidental. Chelating agent class, binds to heavy metals, pulls them from compounds. Industrial application. Remediation or extraction. Depth and distribution pattern inconsistent with surface runoff, this went in intentionally, not as an accident. No way to identify the specific compound without a lab and probably gas chromatography. What I can say. Someone put a compound in that ground that was designed to interact with whatever was there.

Cole set the notebook down.

"You can't name it," he said.

"No. I can tell you what it does to the soil. I can't tell you what it is." Her eyes held his steadily. "I sent the profile description to a pharmacology contact in Bozeman. She said chelating agents at that concentration in soil are used in two contexts, remediation of contaminated sites or extraction of mineral compounds. She didn't know what was in the ground there. She was describing a type."

"And you read?"

She didn't hesitate. "There is nothing in that corridor that requires remediation. It's pack territory. It hasn't been used industrially. So either someone put this there to pull minerals out of the ground, or they put a compound in the ground, and this is what they used to stabilize it." She looked at the map behind him, to the northern corridor. "Either way, someone has been treating that soil deliberately, and they didn't want you to know about it."

Cole was quiet. His gaze moved to the map as it always did, finding the pattern underneath the individual points. The traps. The blinds. The chemical in the ground. Three elements, the same corridor, the same six weeks of professional patience behind all of it.

He had a name for patience that looked like this. He hadn't given it to Lily yet. The full shape of it would require Reid in the territory, and Reid wasn't ready for what lived in the northern corridor to have a name, and Cole wasn't going to give it one before Reid could carry it.

"You've done what we needed," he said. "I want you to keep the notebook. Keep the file open. If anything else comes through the BWR patients that looks related, note it."

"I already am."

He knew. That was the point.

"The corridor," he said. "We're not running it until after the first hard snow. I want the chemical site covered before anyone goes through there in wolf form again."

Her eyes met his. He could see her running the medical read, snow cover as a barrier between soil compound and wolf's nose, reducing respiratory exposure. "Reasonable," she said. Her attention returned to her notebook. "This isn't over."

"No," he said. "It isn't." His gaze returned to the map. "But it doesn't move faster than we do."

He said it with the flat certainty of an Alpha who had been watching his territory for twelve years and, in the deep way of a body that ran in the land it protected, understood that the forces that moved against Blackpine eventually ran into the fact that Blackpine had been here longer. "We hold the ground," his father had said, once. "The ground knows us."

He picked up his coffee. The map said what it always said, patient geometry, the logic of land that had been held deliberately. Someone was working against it. They would find out who, and when they did, the ground would know that too.

After Lily left, he sat with the map for another hour. He hadn't told her what he suspected. He hadn't told Reid yet either, not fully, because telling Reid would require Reid to act on it, and Reid's action in that direction would take him to places Cole wasn't ready to send him. There was a kind of knowing that required the right timing, the same way that Jace's telling of Lily had required it, and this was that kind of knowing.

What Cole knew; the traps, the blinds, the chemical in the ground, and a combination of those three things pointing toward an operation that was too patient and too professional to be local. He had seen this pattern before, or seen the edges of it, in the Oregon pack's dissolution twelve years ago and in the Wyoming incident eighteen years ago that had left Reid the only survivor of twenty-three wolves. He had been twenty-two when his father died, and he had been learning the shape of what was out there ever since, the long shadow that fell across packs that grew visible or grew careless or grew in the wrong direction at the wrong time.

Blackpine hadn't been careless. But it had been growing. And someone had noticed.

He didn't say this in Lily's notebook. He didn't say it on the map. He held it where Alphas held the truths they weren't yet ready to speak, in the bond's deep channel, in the part of him that ran the territory at night and watched the edges, in the long patience of a man who knew the right time to name a threat was when he had the information needed to act on it.

The first snow of December began outside the window. He watched it fall with the full attention he gave to weather, as information, as the territory shifting its season, as the cover that would protect the ground at mile four and buy them the time they needed.

Nora mentioned it on Thursday afternoon, between the supply count and the roster update, sharing details she had catalogued and was passing along as a matter of course.

"The Henderson place finally sold," she said. "The old cabin at the far end of the northern approach road, the one that's been empty since Eleanor Henderson passed. Someone from out of state. Washington, I think. East Coast. Came through a lawyer, remote purchase. Hasn't arrived yet."

Lily noted it. She didn't know the Henderson place. She had heard the name in passing somewhere in the Blackpine information network, as she heard most updates, as a piece of the town's ongoing inventory of itself, the way a small community tracked its property and its people.

She tucked it away and moved on.

Saturday morning Harper Stone-Mercer came into the store at nine-fifteen and sat at the counter and ordered coffee with the ease of a person who had been doing this in the same place long enough to have a way of sitting that was entirely her own.

"I want to have the conversation we haven't had," Harper said. She said it the same way she said most statements, directly, without the social lubricant that most people applied to statements that might be uncomfortable.

Lily poured the coffee. "Which one?"

"The one where you've been here long enough to know what you chose, and I've been here long enough to have a read on it, and neither of us has talked about it properly because there have been other matters going on." Harper wrapped her hands around the mug. "You're pack now. I've been pack for eight months. We should know each other better than we do."

Lily looked at her. Harper Stone-Mercer had a journalist's knack of sitting across from a person, attentive without being intrusive, present without pressing. She had been Cole's mate for months now, settled into her place without performing the settling. Lily had been watching her at pack dinners for six weeks, in the kitchen at HQ, at the long table where Harper did her writing on Sunday mornings. She had been reading Harper the way she read everyone, incrementally, from what was observable.

What was observable was this. Harper Stone-Mercer was sharp and direct in equal measure, and she wore both without contradiction. She had been handed a story that would have broken most people's frameworks and she had absorbed it, reconstructed her understanding, and stayed. She had stayed not because she had no other options but because she had looked at the full picture and made a choice with full information.

Lily knew about that.

Lily set down her mug. Harper had arrived in Blackpine as an investigative journalist with a story to kill. She had ended up staying, had been part of the pack's inner life for months, changed by a place without losing the core that made her herself. Her journalism instinct was operational. She had redirected it.

"What do you want to know?" Lily asked.

"Nothing you don't want to tell me." Harper drank her coffee. "That's not actually how I operate. What I want to say is, it's different from what you expect. Not harder, not easier. Different. The pack bond, the life here, how you stop thinking of yourself as someone who came from somewhere else and start thinking of yourself as someone who is from here." She paused. "It happens before you notice it's happened."

Lily thought about the Sunday morning at the Summit Diner, removing her coat. The craftsmanship of it.

The deliberateness of the arrival.

"I think I noticed it," she said.

"When?"

She considered. "The morning after he told me. I was

on his couch in my coat, watching him make coffee. I knew where the mugs were." Her gaze dropped to her hands on the counter. "I knew them because I'd been reading him for six weeks. I knew where he'd put things before I'd ever been in that room. That's when I knew."

Harper looked at her with the journalist's attention, the one that didn't simplify what it received.

"The town chose you before you chose it," Harper said. "I don't think you had as much agency as you think. But I also think it doesn't matter. You'd have ended up here either way."

Lily considered this. It was possibly true. She had left Blackpine at eighteen because she hadn't had the language for what she was adjacent to, not because she had wanted to leave it. She had been coming back every summer until she stopped coming back, and she had stopped coming back because the coming back had been getting harder in a way she hadn't had words for at twenty-two. She had been heading back the whole time.

"Maybe," she said. "But I still chose it."

"Yes," Harper said. "You did. That's the part that matters."

They drank their coffee. Outside, the northwest sky was doing what it did before serious weather, hardening at the edges, the light going flat. Lily looked at it. A month ago she would have read it as threat. Now she read it as information. She knew the conditions of the pass. She knew the water tower lean. She knew the mountains and what they said.

"He's good," Harper said. Not a question. An affirmation directed at a conclusion she had already assessed and confirmed.

"He is," Lily said.

"Cole took a long time to let anyone in." Harper's gaze drifted to the window. "Jace took longer. Different wound." Her attention returned to Lily. "But they both got there. The Mercer men get there." She smiled as she did when it wasn't the performance of friendliness but the genuine article. "Eventually."

Saturday evening. His cabin.

She had come with the intention that had characterized the Tuesday visit, not because an event required it, not because there was a reason beyond the reason itself. She had wanted to be here. She was here.

This was different from Tuesday. The second time had the quality of two people who already knew what this was, with nothing left to establish and nowhere to perform.

He had made dinner. Real dinner, not what she had made on Saturday, which had been acceptable. This was, venison she knew was from the pack's own hunting in the fall, braised with a sauce that involved red wine and herbs from the labeled jars, and it was food that came from a person who understood that the act of feeding someone was the act of paying attention to them.

She ate it with the complete attention it deserved.

Afterward, the fire, the feel of the cabin in the dark

with the December weather building outside and the stove doing its work and the two of them in the ease of people who were no longer learning each other but are instead deepening what they already know. She had learned, in the four weeks since the cabin at two in the morning, that the ease wasn't the absence of intensity but its refinement; the depths you found when you stopped managing the space between you and stayed in it instead.

She stayed.

In the middle of the night she woke and didn't immediately know where she was. This lasted a heartbeat, the confusion of an unknown ceiling in the shadows, and then she realized, his cabin, his window, the chill of the winter air pressing on the glass. The snow continued to drift down. She could see it in the light from the window, the motion of heavy flakes in still air.

He was asleep beside her, radiating heat. The elevated temperature that had been data was now part of what it was to be near him. She lay in the dark, looked at the ceiling, and thought about what it meant to have a life assembling itself in the voice of right at last, all the pieces arriving in the order they were supposed to arrive.

Blackpine in December. His cabin. The pack. The clinic she was going to build. The north corridor and the question living in it, patient and waiting. The person beside her who had chosen her with his whole self rather than the parts he had allowed.

She wasn't going back to Bozeman. She hadn't been going back to Bozeman for some time. This wasn't a new understanding. It was the most recent version of it, and the most true.

The snow fell outside, covering the ground at mile four and everywhere else. The territory was doing what territories did, turning with the season, holding what it held, being patient as land was patient. She would look at the northern corridor again in the spring, when the snow melted and whatever was in that ground had been through a winter with it. She would add it to the notebook.

For now, the snow, the dark, the steadiness of the person beside her. The ceiling of a cabin she was learning, how it sounded in weather, the beam pattern, the creak above the window when the temperature dropped. She had been cataloging it for weeks without meaning to. This was how belonging worked; you learned the small details about a place, and the specifics became yours, and you didn't notice it happening until it had.

She went back to sleep.

TWENTY-THREE

THE BLIZZARD

The system arrived faster than the forecast had predicted.

Weather in the northern Montana mountains had its own relationship to the forecast, and that relationship mirrored the one the territory had with maps, the map was correct about the general terrain, but the ground held details the map didn't cover. This system had been tracked at forty-eight hours out, then adjusted to thirty-six, and arrived on Monday evening as serious weather arrived, not with announcement but with commitment.

By eight o'clock, the pass was closed. By nine, visibility on the access road had dropped to the range of a truck's headlights. The temperature had fallen twelve degrees in four hours, a drop that had a name in pack knowledge. It killed.

Cole picked up the call at nine-fifteen. Two hikers. A couple in their early thirties, staying in Whitefish, had gone out that morning on the national forest trail system north of the pack boundary. They had told the hotel concierge, out for the day, back by five. The concierge had waited until nine to call, which was too long, but four hours was still within the window.

"They filed a route?" Cole asked.

He was looking at the map while Danny pulled up the trail system on the laptop. The concierge's route description was loose, the northern loop, the viewpoint above the ridge. Three to four hours on a good day. On this day, in this weather, with dark coming, the temperature dropping, and snow blowing horizontal off the mountains, a different calculation entirely.

"Exposed ridge," Reid said, looking at the map. He said it as he said everything, as information, without judgment. The judgment was in what he did next. He was already pulling on his coat.

Cole looked at Jace. Jace was already at the equipment rack. They had run this calculation before, every time a call came in with a combination of timing and weather that made human response times inadequate. Two wolves could cover three miles of exposed terrain in the dark and snow in forty minutes. A human team with equipment in those conditions, two hours minimum, if the road held.

"We go in wolf form until we find them," Cole said. "Clothes cache at the trail junction. You shift back before they see you."

"Got it," Jace said.

Reid was already out the door.

They took the truck. Reid drove. Jace loaded the cache bag—headlamp, emergency kit, the clothes they would need — and they covered the miles to the trailhead in under fifteen minutes. Reid left the engine running when they pulled in. They shifted at the truck and went up into the dark.

THE RIDGE at night in a blizzard was a different place than the mountain in any other condition.

The snow hit the ridge horizontally. The wind carried palpable pressure, as if it were actively resisting any attempt to move through it. Jace's wolf moved with the grace of a creature build for mountain terrain, a thick, insulating coat, balanced weight over sturdy paws, and a center of gravity that anchored it against the shifting terrain. The cold wasn't something to manage. It was information, a constant reading of the environment that his wolf processed as data rather than discomfort.

Reid ran ahead, tracking. This was Reid at his fullest capacity, the pack's tracker in difficult conditions, reading the ground through snow and wind with the hard-earned talent of a man whose entire pack had been killed when he was eighteen and who had spent the eighteen years since becoming unkillable himself, or as close to it as a person could come through skill and attention.

He found the trail. He found where the hikers had left it.

This was the part the human searchers wouldn't have been able to do, the part no map or headlamp or snowshoe covered, the knowledge that the scent of two humans had gone east of the trail at the second viewpoint, probably because the viewpoint was obscured by snow and they had been trying to find it, and that the scent track led to the rock formation three hundred yards east, where two bodies were generating enough heat to be findable.

They were alive. Hypothermic, sheltered in the rock overhang as people sometimes sheltered when they had the sense to stop moving rather than continuing in the wrong direction. They had stopped. That had saved them.

Reid's signal came back through the dark—human voice, already shifted, already dressed. Jace shifted at the clothes cache and covered the last hundred yards on foot, in human form, with the headlamp, the emergency kit, and the voice of a man doing his job.

"Blackpine Wilderness Rescue," he said, coming around the rock. "I've got you."

The woman looked up. Her expression was the expression he had seen before, the one that people had when they had stopped expecting to be found and were adjusting to the fact that they had been, not relief, exactly, but an emotion more complicated than relief, the recalibration of a person returning from somewhere they thought they might not come back from.

"How," she said. Not *thank you.* Not *where did you come from?* Just, *how.* She understood this wasn't a usual response time in a blizzard.

"We know this territory," he said. He gave her the standard answer, the one Cole had developed over years of explaining BWR response times to people who had been found faster than any human team could have found them. "Every foot of it. That's why we're here."

He got them moving. He and Reid each took one, using the technique for supporting a hypothermic person without overloading their cardiovascular system, with the pace calibrated to their condition. He kept his voice steady and his pace consistent, and he didn't say anything that required a response beyond the minimum, because the cardiovascular load of conversation wasn't a burden hypothermic patients needed to carry right now.

The man was in better shape than the woman. He had kept moving longer, which had kept his core temperature higher, which was the paradox of hypothermia, the person who felt worse was often in less danger than the person who felt better because they had stopped feeling anything at all. The woman had the quality that told Lily, when she saw it forty minutes later, that she was in the more serious of the two states.

Back through the timber, where the wind was broken. The snow had drifted across the path in the hour since they had gone in, but not enough to make it impassable. The trees held some of what the ridge hadn't. The mountain's geometry provided shelter where it always did, the knowledge built into Reid's route selection without being explicitly stated because Reid didn't state facts that his body already knew.

The truck was heated. Reid had left it running.

They drove carefully back to HQ. Jace didn't speak. The hikers didn't speak. The blizzard drove at the truck windows, and the road held. A completed rescue settled in the cab, the quality that wasn't celebration but its quieter version, the fact of a job done correctly.

THE CALL from Cole came at nine-thirty.

She was at the store, the upstairs apartment, reading the medical literature on chelating agents that she had pulled from her Bozeman contacts. She answered on the second ring.

"We have two hikers. Hypothermic. ETA forty-five minutes, maybe an hour. Get to HQ."

She was in her coat and out the door in four minutes.

HQ on a call-out was different from HQ at rest. Every light on. Cole at the command table with the radio and the maps. Danny on the laptop, tracking the storm system's movement. The equipment room open.

She went to the supply closet and started pulling what she needed.

Hypothermia protocol. She had done this in the ER, the sequence of warming that didn't shock the cardiovascular system, the monitoring of core temperature recovery, and the watch for afterdrop. She knew the numbers. She knew the signs. She laid out what she had, the two warming blankets from the restocked supply she had been building since week seven, the blood pressure cuff she trusted now, and the thermometer calibrated for shifter baseline that she had acquired and that read human temperatures accurately in the lower range.

She set up two stations at the long table. Heating blankets. IV fluids on the small burner. The protocol in her head, organized as she organized work, in order, by priority, with the contingencies already mapped.

Cole came to the door of the supply area. He watched her work without speaking.

"Twenty minutes," he said.

"I'm ready."

He looked at what she had laid out. He looked at her. "Good," he said.

She understood that he wasn't evaluating her work. He had already evaluated it when she had treated the trail runners. He was confirming, in the Alpha's way, that what he had believed about her when he had said *welcome to BWR* had continued to be accurate. She accepted the confirmation and went back to the protocol.

THEY CAME IN AT TEN-FORTY.

The man had a core temperature of 34.1, and the woman 33.8. Both were coherent but slow, the cognitive effect of moderate rather than severe hypothermia. She assessed them with focused attention, drawing on six years of experience, knowing that the critical window in hypothermia was the rewarming phase, not the cold phase, rewarming too fast was as dangerous as staying cold.

She worked steadily. She talked to them. She told them what she was doing and why. She noted their responses, adjusted her approach when the woman's pressure dropped slightly at the second temperature check and recovered cleanly at the third, and monitored the man's shivering, which was the right kind, productive, the body doing its own work rather than the paralytic absence of shivering that meant the body had given up on the effort.

Cole, Jace, and Reid were in the room but not at the table. Present, giving her space. This was a truth she had come to understand about the pack's management of medical situations; they trusted her. Not provisionally, not like people who were waiting to see how she did. The trust was established.

She kept the hikers for two hours. At one in the morning, both temperatures were stable in the safe range, cognitive clarity was back, and the woman was asking questions about the road conditions and whether she could call her sister.

Lily gave her the phone.

She sat with her empty coffee mug at the end of the long table and felt the quality that came after a good outcome. Not elation, because elation was for people who still needed validation. This was quieter. Professional satisfaction. The job done correctly in conditions that required it.

She had done this six hundred times in Bozeman, approximately. Some of them in better conditions with better equipment and a full team. Some of them in worse conditions with whatever was available and whoever was there. She had been good at it in all of those versions. She was good at it in this version. The setting was different. The medicine wasn't.

Except that it was, slightly. The woman's blood pressure had dropped during recovery and stabilized, which was standard afterdrop and textbook. She had managed it textbook. But the rate of recovery had been faster than textbook, which she had noted and stored without drawing the conclusion she was beginning to draw. The woman was human. There was no biological reason for the rate, unless the environment itself had an effect on it. The pack's territory. The specific characteristic of the air in the HQ building where the pack bond ran at a frequency she couldn't measure with anything she owned. She was adding this to the file.

She was building a file on phenomena that didn't have a medical explanation in the standard framework. It was getting thick. She wasn't alarmed by this. She was interested by it. There was a difference, and she had always been better at the interested version of curiosity. The ER had taught her that. Blackpine was teaching her a different set of interested questions, and she intended to answer all of them.

Reid drove the hikers to Whitefish at one-thirty, which was standard protocol, stable, not critical, hospital for the overnight observation that was prudent even in a positive outcome. Danny went with him to handle the logistics. Cole filed the call.

When the HQ was quiet, Jace sat across from her with two cups of coffee and said nothing, which was the right response.

She wrapped her hands around the mug.

"Both of them will be fine," she said.

"I know." He looked at her steadily. "You do this as the pack runs. Like you were built for it."

She thought about the question of what a person was built for, and whether "built" was the right word, and whether it mattered whether it was built or arrived at through years of training and one very cold November in a forest at two in the morning. She had been heading toward this her whole life. Whether that was design or direction, she couldn't say. It didn't feel important to say.

She drank the coffee. The blizzard leaned into the HQ windows, still committed to its weather. The stove ticked. The building held.

They were the only ones in it.

Later, in the small hours of the night, in the room at the back of HQ that she had understood since October was held in reserve for exactly this kind of situation, she thought about the word built.

He ran hot. He always ran hot. She had always noted this as biology, and she recognized it as biology. It was also the fact of him, the heat of a person who belonged to you in the place that preceded language, a comfort that had nothing to do with temperature and everything to do with the nature of a bond that had been chosen and was choosing back.

She had been afraid, before October, of a kind of permanence. Not of commitment, which she had understood as an intellectual construct. Of the permanence that the mate bond was, the irreversibility of it, the claiming scar that would remain. She had held this at a careful distance in the weeks between the cabin and the clearing, not running from it but not arriving at it either. She had been doing the thing she did, waiting for the picture to complete, not forcing the conclusion before the data was in.

The data was in. Had been for a while.

She lay in the quiet of a building that had weathered the night and was still standing, as it always was, as this pack always was, and she saw that permanence wasn't what she had been afraid of. What she had been afraid of was the permanent choice being the wrong choice.

It wasn't the wrong choice.

She wasn't afraid of it.

Outside, the blizzard was ending as Montana weather ended, not apologetically, not gradually, but by simply stopping. One moment the wind and the next a stillness, the complete absence of the noise the storm had been making, the quiet of a mountain landscape that had received a great deal of snow and was now holding it.

She listened to the stillness and the steady presence beside her. The territory was out there in the dark, the pack somewhere in it, and she could feel something of that. Peripheral, not yet named, the outline of a thing she was going to know well. Outside, the territory held its new snow, white and clean, covering mile four and the eastern corridor and everywhere else the territory ran. She went to sleep.

TWENTY-FOUR

THE CLINIC

She proposed the clinic framework on Thursday afternoon.

Not a formal presentation. She wasn't a person who gave formal presentations. She had spent Tuesday and Wednesday after the blizzard writing down what she needed, crossing out what she could get by without, and rebuilding the list from the floor up rather than from the ceiling down. The result was a piece of paper with five items, three of which were non-negotiable and two of which were aspirational. She brought the non-negotiable ones to Cole.

She sat across the map table. Cole was a man who responded to directness, so she gave him that. She read the three items aloud.

"I need regular access to a lab for basic bloodwork. Not the full hospital panel, not anything that requires a standing account. I need to be able to run a CBC and a basic metabolic without anyone asking which practice it's billed to."

Cole listened.

"I need a locked supply space in the HQ that's mine. The shelf in the closet isn't adequate anymore. I need refrigeration for some of what I'm starting to build."

"There's a room off the equipment bay," he said. "It's been used for storage. We can clear it."

"I need an understanding with the rotating doctor." Her eyes returned to the list. "Dr. Vasquez, the one who comes in from Whitefish twice a month. He and I need to have a direct conversation about what I'm doing and how we're going to work together. I've been running informal assessments for weeks now. That needs to be formal."

Cole studied her. "He doesn't know about the pack."

"He doesn't need to know about the pack. He needs to know there's a nurse in Blackpine who handles the cases a rotating doctor can't cover between visits. That's a true statement that doesn't require the rest."

He was quiet. "What else?"

"That's it," she said. "For now."

His gaze moved to the paper, then to her. The Alpha's assessment was thorough and unhurried. She had been on the receiving end of it since November and had stopped finding it anything but efficient. He was reading whether she had thought this through, which she had, and whether she understood what she was building, which she did.

"The room is yours," he said. "I'll talk to Reid about the cold storage. Call Vasquez whenever you're ready."

She called him that evening.

Dr. Vasquez had been doing the Blackpine rotation for three years. He was a practical man who had long since stopped being surprised by what small Montana communities improvised between his visits. She had looked him up before she called, board-certified in emergency medicine, with rural health rotations during his residency, and the Blackpine doctor by choice rather than assignment because he had grown up in a small town in eastern Montana and understood what the absence of consistent medical coverage did to a community over time.

When Lily described what she was proposing, he listened without interrupting. She had been a nurse long enough to understand what a doctor's silence during a presentation meant. His silence was that of someone taking notes.

When she finished, he said, without ceremony, "The town has needed this for two years. When can you start?"

She laughed. "I already have."

He laughed. She liked him immediately. She told him about the BWR supply room, the protocol she had been building, and the cases she had managed in the past six weeks. She didn't tell him about the pack. She didn't need to. The cases she described were all human-adjacent or abstracted enough to be medically accurate without requiring the biological specifics of what the pack was.

They agreed to meet the following week, when he was in Blackpine for his regular rotation. He wanted to see the space. She wanted to show it to him.

"One thing," she said, before they hung up.

"Name it."

"I will handle what I handle," she said. "I won't refer anything to you that I can manage. But when I do refer a case, I need you to trust that I have assessed it correctly and that the history you're getting is accurate even if it's not complete."

A pause. "That's how I work with every community health worker I've ever partnered with. If you're good at this, I won't need the complete history."

"I'm good at this," she said.

"I believe you," he said. "Good night, Lily."

She told Earl at the store on Friday morning, before opening.

He was at the register with the morning mail when she came down and said, directly, that she had arranged to begin working as the town's nurse in collaboration with Dr. Vasquez, that she would use a space at BWR for medical work requiring equipment, and that the rotating clinic sessions in Blackpine would begin in January.

Earl sorted a piece of mail. He sorted another piece. He put the stack down.

"Your grandmother always said," he said, "that you were going to do important work in this town."

This was the most words Earl had used in a single statement in her recent memory. Her gaze settled on him.

"She said it when you were twelve," he said. "After the summer, you asked her twelve questions about the Mercer boys in a single afternoon, and she'd had to answer all of them without telling you the truth you were actually asking." He picked up his coffee mug. "I told her she was projecting. She told me I was wrong."

"Were you wrong?"

"Mm," Earl said. In the tone that meant, *yes, and I've been sitting with that for fifteen years, and you don't need me to say it more clearly than that.*

She went behind the counter, and they opened the store.

She told Dottie at noon, when Dottie came downstairs for tea. Dottie listened with her hands wrapped around her mug and her eyes on Lily's face, and the expression of a woman who had been waiting for a sentence to be said for a long time and was receiving it correctly.

"Good," Dottie said.

That was all. It was enough.

FRANK CALLED FRIDAY EVENING, the regular call.

She had been expecting it as she always expected it, with the consistency of a call that had been reliable since she moved to Bozeman at twenty-two and that had shifted in tone since she came to Blackpine, each call a slightly different calibration of what he knew and what he was sitting with.

"How's the weather?" he said.

"Bad. We had a blizzard on Monday. The pass was closed for two days."

"I heard about that." He hadn't heard from her. He had heard from the weather service, or the highway report, or some mechanism of paternal monitoring; she didn't need to understand the full shape to accept it as his form of love. "BWR had a call."

"Two hikers," she said. "Both fine."

A pause. "You were there."

"I treated them. At the HQ." She let this sit, as she now let statements sit with her father, not pushing, not filling the silence. Just letting him receive.

"Good," he said. The same word Earl had used. The same frequency, even, the one that contained a complete assessment and had decided that the word was sufficient.

"The clinic," she said. "I'm starting one."

She told him about Vasquez. About the room at BWR. About the arrangement. She told him plainly, as she told Cole facts, because her father was a county assessor and processed information best when it was organized.

When she finished, he was quiet.

"Your grandmother's mother," he said at last, "was the one who ran the informal clinic here in the forties, before Blackpine had a proper doctor. She did it out of the back of the general store." He paused. "I found that in the county records. The notation is from a public health survey in 1948."

She hadn't known this. She absorbed it the way she absorbed everything, as data, filed without forcing it. Except that this piece was different. This wasn't about the Mercers or the land trust or the pack. This was her own family, the Thornton thread running through Blackpine's history, parallel and adjacent to the Mercer thread, finally converging.

Earl's mother had known about the Mercers before anyone told her. Dottie's mother had run the town's informal clinic in the 1940s. Each generation of this family had arrived at the same truth through the same route, by paying attention, by refusing to leave a question unresolved, and by staying. She was the fourth.

"I thought you should know," he said. "Seemed relevant."

Her gaze drifted to the ceiling of the store's back room, to the shelves she had reorganized in her first week, at the space that had been her family's for generations. She thought about Earl's mother knowing what the Mercers were before anyone told her. She thought about Dottie's mother running the clinic from the back of the store a decade before Lily was born. She thought about the fact that she had come back in October telling herself it was temporary, and had reorganized the shelves in her first week anyway.

"Thank you," she said. "That is relevant."

Another pause. His breathing; the sound of a man who had more to say and was deciding whether to say it.

"Are you happy?" he asked. The same question he had asked when he stood in the store in November with the folder on the counter. She understood now that this was his real question, the one underneath all the records research and the Friday calls and the nineteen years of protective precision. The one he hadn't known how to ask until she had given him enough to work with.

"Yes," she said. "I am."

"Good," he said. And then, in a pitch she hadn't heard from him in years, a warmth that wasn't managed data or functional concern, unguarded. "I'm glad."

She held the phone after she hung up, looked out the window at the December dark, and thought about how a man who loved badly could learn to love better, and about the patience that required in the people who loved him back.

She had that patience. She had always had it. She was her father's daughter. She was also her grandmother's granddaughter, and her great-grandmother's great-granddaughter, and the shape of a family that had been in this town for three generations, doing the same work in different ways, paying attention, holding secrets in trust, staying.

She put the phone down and went back to the store.

Mrs. Patterson was at the counter, which was where she often was at this hour. She had her supplement bag, her weekly news, and the look of a woman who had been watching Lily Thornton for ten weeks and had formed a complete opinion she didn't feel the need to fully articulate because she had said the important part on the first day.

Mrs. Patterson had been right on the first day and every day since, and Lily understood now what it had cost her to say only that much and no more.

She rang up the supplements and listened to the news about the water tower, which was now definitively going to be addressed in the spring. Mrs. Patterson had been told by the mayor, who had told her at the community meeting last week, which Lily hadn't attended because she had been at BWR reorganizing the supply room.

"You should come to the next one," Mrs. Patterson said. "The meeting. You're a permanent resident now."

She said it as she might have said the water tower leans three degrees, a fact that had already incorporated. *Not, are you planning to stay. Not, is this permanent.* A statement of fact that the town had already incorporated.

"I'll be there," Lily said.

Mrs. Patterson picked up her bag. At the door, she paused, as she did when she had one more statement to deliver. "Your grandmother approves," she said. "She always said this town needed someone like you."

Lily looked at her. Mrs. Patterson nodded once and left, the bell shrieking behind her.

Saturday evening at his cabin had the settled quality of a week that had gone right, a rescue, a clinic arrangement, and a Frank call that had reached somewhere new, the steady accumulation of a life running right.

She wasn't bringing urgency. Neither was he.

The fourth time had the quality of a connection fully arrived at, the ease of two people who were no longer learning each other in this way but deepening it, the same way they deepened everything, with attention, with patience, without performing anything they didn't feel. She had noted, as a clinical observation she was eventually going to stop calling clinical, that the warmth of him was unchanged, the character of his stillness was unchanged, and the thing he brought to this that she didn't have a word for was unchanged. She was learning what it was to be chosen by someone who chose with his whole self rather than the parts he allowed.

She stayed. She woke in the gray early morning to the stillness that followed snow, the world outside held in the quiet of fresh accumulation, the light through the cabin window at the soft edge of dawn.

His flannel shirt was on the chair.

She put it on. It was warm and too big, and it smelled of the forest, the clean cold of the altitude, and him. She stood in the cabin in the early morning wearing it, dressed for the morning in what was available, and it suited her.

She went to the kitchen and started the coffee. Her gaze drifted to the window, to the December morning as it brewed; the pines with their snow load, what it was like to have the light at this hour through the mountain cold, the sky beginning its pale shift from dark to gray to the pale winter blue it would be by nine. She knew this sky now. She had been learning it since she arrived, the Blackpine sky in its various moods, how it announced the weather, the temperature, and the character of the day ahead.

He came out of the bedroom at seven already knowing she was up before he opened his eyes, the pack bond telling him direction and presence even in sleep. He stopped in the doorway, his eyes finding her in his shirt in his kitchen.

Her eyes met his.

"Coffee's ready," she said.

He sat at the table, and she brought him a mug and sat across from him. They didn't say anything for a while, which was the texture of a morning between two people who had been talking to each other for three months and had found the place where silence was also conversation.

The mountains were out through the kitchen window. White and clear and entirely present. She had been looking at these mountains for three months. She was going to keep looking at them.

"What are you thinking?" he said.

"That I'm glad I came back," she said. She had said this before, in the clearing, in the dark. It was still true. It was more true, as some truths became more true over time rather than less.

"I'm glad you came back," he said.

She drank her coffee. Outside, a jay landed on the snow-covered porch rail, looked at the window, and flew off. The morning did its morning work, light increasing, cold holding, the day gathering itself. She had nowhere to be until the store opened at ten, and neither did he.

They stayed at the kitchen table.

TWENTY-FIVE

THE CLEARING

Jace had been thinking about how to do it since October.

He knew the truth the moment she turned on the step stool, an instinctive recognition, like a wolf's. The bond formed easily, but he spent weeks grasping its meaning. The challenge lay not in the truth itself but in how to navigate it. The how of it was what mattered. This was the path he had been carefully shaping for three months.

He hadn't planned Saturday. He had planned the week before, and the week before that, running the question against the specifics of December, the weather, the pack's schedule, and the state of what was between them. He had been looking for the right day as he looked for movement in the territory, not at the most obvious point but at the point where the conditions were best.

Saturday morning, she sat across from him in his kitchen, wearing his flannel shirt, with her coffee and her morning ease of a person who had nowhere to be and was satisfied by that. He understood that the day was today.

Not because of the shirt. Not because of the morning, specifically. Because he had been watching her for three months and had learned to read her as he read what he cared about, not from the surface but from the accumulation, the long picture. And the long picture said she is ready. Not waiting. Ready.

He asked her at ten, after she had dressed and before she went to open the store.

"Tonight," he said. "The clearing."

Her eyes met his. He held the gaze. She read what she needed from it, and he read what he needed from her face, the nurse's assessment and then the other awareness underneath it, the part that wasn't clinical and never had been.

"What time?" she asked.

"After dark. Seven."

She nodded. She picked up her coat. She went to open the store.

He stood in the cabin after she left and felt the weight of a day that had been decided. His wolf was the quietest it had been since October, since the moment she had arrived in pack territory and recognition had flooded through the bond like a signal too clear to mistake. Not the eager anticipation he had been carrying for months. A deeper certainty. The settled nature of completion approaching.

He called Cole.

Cole answered on the second ring.

"Tonight," Jace said.

A pause. "Good." Just that. The Alpha receiving information that had been expected and confirming it was the right information. "I'll let the pack know."

The pack bond would tell them anyway, as it told them what mattered, not in words but in the resonance of a change that was happening, the frequency of the bond when it was about to change. They would know without being told. Cole's message was courtesy rather than necessity, as Blackpine did most rituals, formally, because the form mattered, even when the substance was already understood.

"Don't come to the clearing," Jace said.

"I know," Cole said. He said it in the tone that meant, *this is yours. We are here. We aren't there.*

He put the phone down and went to build a fire in the woodstove and make himself useful for the rest of the day, which was harder than it sounded.

The cabin was clean. The firewood was stacked. The kitchen was organized as he had been keeping it since September, every item in its place, the deliberate domestic order of a man who had decided how to live and was living it. He had nothing to do except wait, and waiting wasn't his skill. His skill was motion, running the territory, tracking the edges, and doing the work the pack required. Stillness was Cole's domain. Jace did stillness badly.

He went outside and walked the perimeter of the property in human form, checking the fence line he had rebuilt in October, the woodshed he had restacked after the first snow, the details of a place that had been his project since Amanda and was now entirely completed. He found nothing that needed doing. He went back inside.

Harper had told him, at last Sunday's dinner, that Cole had been the same way before the claiming. "He couldn't sit still," she had said. "Kept finding items to repair that didn't need repairing. Rewired the same lamp twice." She had looked at him with the journalist's assessment, the one that didn't simplify what it received. "The waiting is the hard part. The moment itself is easy."

He understood what she meant now.

SHE HAD LEARNED about the claiming that night in his cabin, sitting at his kitchen table at two in the morning with her hands around a coffee mug, learning what she was agreeing to.

She had asked, *What does it feel like.* He had said, *Permanent. Not painful. The bond completes.*

She had asked about the scar. He had said, *It stays. A crescent, from the bite. It heals clean.*

She had asked, *Does it hurt.*

Yes. Briefly. And then it doesn't.

She had filed all of it. She had been filing it for three months.

She had asked about the ceremony because she was a nurse and needed the clinical picture before she could approach it as a person. She had the clinical picture. She had carried it since November. It hadn't frightened her.

What she had needed, after the clinical picture, was time to accept it, not analyze it.

Three months was the right amount of time. She had known this as she knew diagnoses before the full data was in, with the bodily certainty that preceded language, the sense of a picture completing before the last piece arrived.

The last piece had arrived this morning in his kitchen.

She closed the store at five. She didn't tell Earl where she was going. She didn't need to. His gaze found her when she came down after changing into the heavier coat, the one she had bought in November when Mrs. Kowalski had recommended the brand. His expression was the expression of a man who had been holding this in trust for thirty years and was watching the trust discharge.

"Go," he said, in the same tone Dottie had used on the Sunday morning when Lily told her what was happening. The voice of a family that had been part of this story longer than she had known there was one.

She drove to his cabin at six-thirty.

The road was clear. The December weather had held for three days, with no new accumulation, a pause between systems that the locals knew how to use. She drove with the attention she gave the task, steady, present, not rushing what didn't need rushing.

He was on the porch when she pulled up. She could see him in the headlights. The silhouette of a man who had been waiting for a car to arrive and was now watching it arrive. He came down the steps as she parked. He opened her door.

"Hey," he said.

"Hey," she said.

They stood by her car in the cold December dark. The pines were tall and still around the clearing. The cabin glowed behind him, the windows lit, the feel of a place that was waiting for the night to begin.

"Walk?" he asked.

"Walk," she agreed.

The clearing his father had brought him to was fifteen minutes along the trail he had shown her in November, through the trees. She had walked it once before, on a Sunday afternoon, learning the shape of the land as she learned, by going through it, by putting her body in the space. She knew the route now. She fell into step beside him, and they walked without speaking, the snow crunching under their boots, the cold sharp, clean, and serious.

THE SKY above the tree line was clear, the stars beginning where the mountains stopped, the arrangement of the December sky over northern Montana, Orion, the Pleiades, the river of the Milky Way across the dark.

She had been looking up more. This was a habit she hadn't had in Bozeman, not regularly, not with the attention that turned looking into knowing. She had been learning the Blackpine sky as she had been learning, incrementally, by accumulation, until it became hers.

She stood at the center of the clearing with him. The mountains to the north, as they always were. The territory below the clearing, the pack somewhere in it, the bond she couldn't yet feel but understood was there, was always there, the frequency the land ran at.

He looked at the mountains, then at her.

"Ready?" he asked.

She studied him. Sandy-brown hair. Brown eyes with the steady quality she had been cataloging since October, the one that, in certain lights, had the amber undertone she had spent weeks trying to name. The heat of him in the cold, the same heat she had noted the first moment he caught her on the icy steps and had been learning the meaning of ever since.

The person who had come into a store to buy the wrong batteries because he had needed a reason to be there. The person who had rebuilt a cabin with his hands and chosen the cleaning products that went under the sink with precision, having decided how to live and living that way. The person who had called her from a forest floor at ten o'clock at night because she was who he wanted to call. The person who had said, *I choose you. Not because the bond says so. Because I mean it.*

She had chosen him too. She was choosing him now, in the clearing his father had brought him to when he was nine, in the December cold with the mountains watching and the pack somewhere in the territory below, a decision that was permanent and deserved to be.

"Ready," she said.

〜

WHAT SHE HADN'T FULLY grasped from the clinical description was the character of the moment before.

He had his hand at the side of her face, his palm fever-hot against her cheek, and she could feel what it was to have his attention on her, the whole of it, undivided, the man without the wall. His eyes in the dark held the amber she had spent weeks trying to name, fully lit now, the gleam of the bond's recognition, nothing supernatural, nothing she couldn't have rationalized away if she hadn't known what it was. She knew what it was.

The claiming bite was to the neck. She had known this. She knew the mechanics. She tilted her head, held still, and trusted the three months of evidence she had accumulated, that he was who he was, that this was what she had chosen, that the permanent bond wasn't frightening when it was the right choice.

The partial shift, she felt it, the change in the pressure of his hand, and then the bite, which was exactly what he had said it would be. Yes it hurt, briefly, and then it didn't. The bond completed with a sensation she had no clinical word for, a resonance that wasn't sound and wasn't feeling, and was both, the sensation of a door opening between two people who had been standing on opposite sides of it for three months.

She felt him. Not just the heat and the presence. His heartbeat, as clearly as she felt her own. His emotion in this moment, which wasn't a word and was everything. The wave of it, the relief, the certainty, and the current underneath, both of which had been running since October without a name and had one now.

Ours, she thought. And then, understanding,*mine.*

Yours, the bond answered. Not a voice. Not language. Just the bond, telling her what she already knew.

He pulled back. His eyes found hers, in the dark, the amber gold of them, the look she had been cataloging, now with the full picture of it, the person who had guarded himself for six years and had decided not to, not with her.

She could feel the pack through it. Not close. Not present. A background frequency, the bond she was now part of in a different way than she had been an hour ago. Cole, somewhere in the territory, was a steady presence within the new awareness. The others, further, the signatures she was beginning to recognize without yet having names for all of them.

She touched the claiming mark at her neck. It would scar. He had told her this. She had filed it. She was glad it would.

"There," he said. His voice, low and even, was the voice he used when he was saying the truth from the center of himself.

"There," she agreed.

They stood in the clearing with the mountains and the stars and the cold that reached her through every layer and didn't reach him at all, and she leaned into the heat of him, and he put his arm around her, and they were quiet for a while.

The territory was quiet. The pack bond hummed at its low frequency, fuller now, with a new note added that hadn't been there before. She was learning to read it, the same way she had learned, by attention, by increments. Cole's signature was low in the bond, steady and deep. Harper was near him. The others were farther, the shapes she would come to know by name over the weeks ahead.

The mountains were there, the same mountains that had been there her whole life, the same mountains she had been looking at through the store window since October.

She was on the right side of everything.

After a while, they walked back. The trail through the trees was easier in the dark than it had been in November, or she knew it better, or both. He walked beside her with the ease of a man who had spent the last three months waiting for this and was no longer waiting. She could feel that too now, his emotion running alongside her own, the bond telling her what she would have known anyway, but more clearly, more immediately.

Good, she thought. And felt the agreement come back, not a word, not language, but the resonance of a feeling shared.

They went back to the cabin. They went inside. The fire was burning low in the woodstove, the kitchen light was on, and the place met them like it had been waiting. He took her coat off slowly, his fingers lingering at her throat where the claiming mark was fresh, then kissed her there with a care that turned into hunger almost immediately.

This time there was no uncertainty left to work through and no barrier left standing between them. She undressed him with the same focus she brought to what mattered, wanting the full reality of him under her hands. He answered in kind, patient only until patience stopped making sense. When they found the bed, they took each other with the fierce relief of people who had spent months earning the right to stop holding back.

Afterward, she lay against his chest and listened to the new bond settle quiet and deep between them, no longer a promise or a theory. It was simply there, as solid as the cabin around them and the winter night outside.

She was part of it now. She was going to keep being part of it.

Outside, the December night was cold, clear, and quiet. The pack bond hummed at its new frequency, and she learned to listen to it, and it was right.

TWENTY-SIX

DECEMBER

He woke before dawn the morning after the claiming, and she was there.

Not extraordinary. She had stayed before. The cabin had her shape in it by now, the presence of a second person in the space, the shift in the air that came from two people breathing instead of one. He had known this before he opened his eyes. The pack bond told him her location and emotional state, as it had always told him the pack's, not in words or not in pictures, but in the bodily knowledge of a bond you were part of.

What was different now was the character of it. The bond with Lily was its own frequency, distinct from the pack and part of it at the same time. He had known it would be there. He had told her what the claiming bond did, had described it plainly and specifically in October, had known the mechanics of it since he was old enough to understand what the mate bond was. He hadn't fully understood what it would feel like until it was.

She was asleep. Her breathing was even. Her emotional state was the clear, uncomplicated state of sleep, no processing, no filing, just rest. He lay in the dark and read it as he had been learning to read her, with attention, without forcing.

This was going to be the baseline now. The steadiness of her beside him and the bond telling him she was present. He had spent six years behind the wall he'd built, and it had done what he'd needed it to do, and it was no longer necessary. He was going to have to learn a different architecture. He was ready to.

He got up carefully, as he had learned to move around her in the mornings when she was sleeping, quiet, deliberate, the wolf's instinct for silence useful in domestic settings. She didn't wake. He watched her from the doorway. The curve of her shoulder under the quilt, the strawberry-blonde curls against the pillow, the stillness of a woman who slept soundly because she felt safe. Then he went to start the coffee.

The kitchen was cold. December in the cabin meant the woodstove needed attention first, which he gave it. Kindling, then the smaller splits, then he closed the door and the draft adjusted. The routine of it was satisfying, as all competent routines were. He had been performing this sequence since he was twelve, when his father had taught him how the cabin worked, what it needed, and how to keep it through a Montana winter.

He stood at the window while the coffee brewed. The mountains were there as they always were, completely, without comment. The December light was beginning to show at the eastern edge, that characteristic of pre-dawn that wasn't yet color but was no longer full dark. He had seen this light ten thousand times. He was going to keep seeing it.

The coffee finished. He poured two mugs and brought one back to the bedroom. She was awake now. He had felt the shift in the bond before he saw her eyes open, that transition from sleep to waking that he could now track without looking.

"Coffee," he said.

She took the mug. Her eyes met his over the rim with the direct, clinical attention she brought to tasks, and he felt through the bond that she was doing what she did, cataloging, assessing, and filing. Reading him, as she always did.

"You're different," she said.

He was. He sat on the edge of the bed. "You can feel it."

"I can feel it." She said it with the precision of a woman still learning the parameters of a new system. "It's not what I expected."

"What did you expect?"

She considered the question as she considered all questions, thoroughly, without rushing. "Noise. Intensity. Overwhelm I would have to manage." Her gaze dropped to the mug in her hands. "It's not that. It's just—there. Like having another sense."

He nodded. That was what it was. The mate bond didn't demand attention. It provided information, constant and quiet, as the pack bond did. She would learn to stop noticing it consciously, as he had stopped noticing the pack bond decades ago. It would become part of the background structure of her awareness.

"It gets quieter," he said.

"I don't mind the volume," she said. "I'm just learning the frequency."

She would. She learned everything.

He was at the map table when Cole arrived at eight.

Cole came in with the economy of a man who had been up since five and was operating at full capacity without announcing it. His gaze swept the map, then settled on Jace. The Alpha's read on a pack member took about two seconds.

"Good," Cole said.

That was the whole conversation. It was the right amount. Cole sat across from him, and they worked through the morning patrol report the way they always did, methodically, without hurrying, the two of them reading the territory from what the patrol data said and what it didn't. The northern corridor was quiet. The blinds were still in place, neither approached nor acknowledged. Reid had confirmed their position unchanged three days ago. Cole's order stood, watch, don't confront, not yet.

The professional watcher was still out there. The question of who and why remained unanswered. Cole's position hadn't changed since the first blind was found. Patience, observation, the long game. The pack could afford to wait. The watcher, whoever they were, had shown no sign of hostile intent. Only interest. Interest could be managed. Eventually, when the time was right, it could be understood.

The pack bond was fuller than it had been yesterday. Cole felt it too. Jace could tell from how the Alpha's attention settled over the bond with the satisfaction of completion, a circuit closed, a bond that had been building for three months resolved into its right shape.

Neither of them said anything about that either.

Harper came in around ten with coffee, the energy of a woman who had been writing since six and needed to be around other humans for a while. She sat at the far end of the table with her laptop and didn't interrupt them. This was how it worked. The HQ was a space where the pack moved through each other's orbits without requiring constant acknowledgment.

MONDAY MORNING, she called Dr. Vasquez.

She had been planning this call since the blizzard. She had the room at BWR cleared and stocked, and the refrigeration unit scheduled for delivery next week. She had the protocol she'd been building since week seven, refined through the informal cases and the specific education required to learn a new patient population. What she needed was the formal arrangement, not a practice, not an official clinic, but a standing relationship with the rotating doctor that would make her presence in Blackpine's medical landscape official rather than informal.

Vasquez answered on the second ring. He remembered her from their previous conversation. He had been thinking about the proposal, he said.

"I've talked to a few people," he said. "People who know Blackpine. They all say the same thing."

"What's that?"

"That the town has needed this for years." He said it plainly, as fact. "The question was never whether. It was who?"

She told him about the room. About the supply base she had built over eleven weeks. About the cases she had managed informally. She described them in clinical, abstract language, accurate without requiring context the doctor didn't have. The fever patient in October. The hypothermia case from the first snowfall. The various injuries and chronic management issues that had found their way to her because word had spread as it does in small towns, quietly, completely, without announcement.

He listened as he took notes, not interrupting.

When she finished, he replied, "I'll come to Blackpine next Thursday. I want to see the setup."

"I'll be there," she said.

"I know you will," he said. There was a quality in his voice that sounded like respect, or recognition, or both. "That's why this is going to work."

She hung up and sat with the phone in her hand. It had changed the shape of the next several years of her life.

She sat with it and waited for it to feel larger than it did. It didn't. It fit.

She went downstairs.

Earl was at the counter with the afternoon mail. His gaze lifted. It moved to her face.

"Tea," he said, moving toward the kettle.

She sat at the counter. He made the tea as Earl made it, unhurried and correct, without asking how she wanted it because he had known since she was six. The kettle whistled. He poured. He set a mug in front of her and sat across from her with his.

She told him about Vasquez. About the clinic. About the room at BWR and what it was going to become.

Earl listened with the patience of a man who had held this store and this family for fifty years and understood that what was being said to him was more than medical logistics. He wrapped both hands around his mug. The afternoon light came through the front windows, catching the dust motes in the air, the same light she had been watching since she was a child, the character of December in the general store.

"Good," he said. The same word Cole had used, in the same tone. The one that meant, *I have been waiting for this, and you did it, and that is all that needs to be said.*

She went upstairs and told Dottie.

Dottie was at the window with her book, the stronger left hand holding the cover, the weaker right hand braced on the armrest as she braced it now. Not compensating. Just existing in the body she had. The stroke had taken some abilities from her. It hadn't taken her ability to see clearly, to understand what she was seeing, or to communicate that understanding in the Dottie way that had never required many words.

She listened to the whole of it.

When Lily finished, Dottie said, "Mm."

It was the *mm* that meant, *I knew before you did, and I am glad you caught up, and this is how it was always going to go.*

Lily sat with her grandmother and looked out the window at the mountains. Three generations of Thornton women had looked at this view. She was the one who would stay.

Friday evening, Frank called.

She had told him about the clinic on Tuesday. Not everything, just the shape of it. The arrangement with Vasquez, the room at BWR, and the supply base she had been building. He had listened the way he listened to information, taking it in, running it against his model of the situation, and filing it for later processing. He had returned the next day with a question she hadn't anticipated, because that was what Frank did; he processed, and then he asked the question that showed he had been processing.

The question he asked, "Is this what you went to Bozeman for?"

She thought about it. "No," she said. "It's what I came back for."

A long pause. She could hear him breathing on the other end of the line, Frank working through something the way he always worked through something, not rushing it. She didn't fill it. Neither did he.

Then, in the voice Frank used when he was saying words he had been holding for a long time, "Your grandmother always said you were going to do work that mattered in that town." He stopped. "I thought she was being sentimental."

"She wasn't," Lily said.

"No," he said. "She wasn't."

She held the phone and listened to the silence on his end. It wasn't the silence of a man withholding. It was the silence of a man who had run out of arguments and, on the other side of that, had found a state that had the shape of acceptance. Frank Thornton didn't do acceptance quickly or gracefully. He did it by examining it from every angle until he couldn't find a flaw in it.

"I'll come," he said. "In the spring. I'd like to see the clinic."

"I'd like that," she said.

She meant it.

~

Friday was pack dinner.

The same as always, Nora's food, Old Tom's story,

Danny's commentary, Eli's running argument with Danny about something no one else had followed closely enough to adjudicate, Reid at the far end with his coffee and his watchful quiet. The long table with its wear. The ring where Old Tom's mug always went, the scorch mark from a candle incident three years ago that nobody had ever explained, the grain of the wood she had been looking at for weeks and had stopped noticing as new. Harper at Cole's left, the laptop closed for once because Friday dinner was the one time Harper put away the work. Jace beside Lily, the heat of him in the chair.

She was at the table as Harper was at the table. She had been at the table this way since November, occupying it without performing the occupation, knowing where the water pitcher went and who got served first and which stories were coming before they arrived. But this Friday was different from those Fridays in one way that she could feel and the pack could feel, and none of them mentioned it because it didn't need to be.

The bond. Hers and Jace's, the new frequency in the pack's overall hum, the frequency that completed a shape that had been building for months. She could feel Cole's steady depth at one end of the table, the others at their various distances, and Jace right beside her at the center of it, and it was all one whole. Not complicated. Not loud. Just present, as the truths that were right were present, without requiring acknowledgment.

The food was venison stew, Nora's winter standard, rich and filling as December food was supposed to be. The bread was fresh. Sarah had baked it that afternoon, as Sarah baked bread every Friday because that was how the pack worked, everyone contributing what they contributed. The wine was from the case Cole kept in the back, nothing expensive, just red and adequate and present.

Old Tom's story arrived in the third act of dinner, which was where it always arrived. She had heard three versions of the grizzly story now. This one had a new detail, a specific type of berry involved in the initial encounter, which Old Tom had added since last week for reasons he didn't explain. Danny pointed this out. Old Tom looked at him with the serene patience of a man of seventy-eight who had been dealing with Danny Cruz for years and had reached a settled position on the matter. Reid, at the far end, looked at the middle distance with great concentration and said nothing.

She laughed. It wasn't a polite laugh, the kind she had been producing in the first weeks. It was the laugh of a person at home.

Jace's hand found hers under the table. Not demonstrative. Just there. The bond told her what she already knew, that he was content, that he was where he wanted to be, that this evening was the life he had been building toward since she arrived. Ordinary, easy, entirely itself.

She squeezed his hand. She didn't need to say anything. The bond said it.

〜

SHE DROVE HOME through the December dark.

The mountains were invisible, the sky heavy with what the forecast said was incoming weather. She had learned to read this sky by now. The character of the overcast that preceded serious snowfall was different from the light cloud cover that came and went without consequence. There would be snow by morning. She would wake to it, as she had woken to it through November and now through December, the rhythm of a Montana winter she was learning by paying attention.

She parked behind the store, in the space that had been hers since she arrived in October. She turned off the engine and sat in the quiet, not thinking about Bozeman. She wasn't thinking about what came next. She was thinking about a place that held you as Blackpine held, not gently, not carefully, but completely.

She went inside.

The kettle was on. Earl had left it on the low setting he used when he knew she'd be coming back late. The stove ticked in the corner, the cast-iron working through its cooling cycle, the sound of a building settling into its winter rhythms. The bell above the door announced her arrival the way it always had. She wasn't going to oil it. The shriek was part of the store. The store was part of her.

She made herself a cup of tea from the water Earl had left warming. She stood in the kitchen she had known since she was six and looked out the window at the December dark. The mountains were out there, invisible but present. The territory was out there too. She could feel it through the pack bond, the way she could feel the pack members at their various locations. Jace at his cabin. Cole at the main house. The others in their places, the geography of a family that wasn't defined by blood but by bonds older than blood.

She belonged to this. It belonged to her.

She finished her tea. She went upstairs. She was home.

AN EXCERPT FROM: SHADOW'S MATE
THE WOLVES OF BLACKPINK BOOK 3

The rental car's tires hummed over cracked asphalt as Zara Washington passed the faded green sign.

BLACKPINE, MONTANA.
POPULATION 2,400.
ELEVATION 4,847 FT.

Her phone had lost signal twenty minutes earlier. The GPS had died with it, leaving her with a hand-drawn map she'd found in her mother's kitchen drawer, tucked between expired coupons and a grocery list dated 2019. Her mother's handwriting was neat, precise, and familiar.

Her mother was dead.

Zara blinked and forced her attention back to the road. Exhaustion had become a physical weight behind her eyes, making the afternoon light feel too sharp. She hadn't slept properly since the funeral. Hadn't eaten much either, though she couldn't remember whether she'd had breakfast this morning or just stared at a granola bar until it was time to leave.

The town unfolded ahead of her in pieces. A leaning water tower painted with the name *BLACKPINE* in letters that had faded to ghosts of themselves. A general store with a hand-lettered sign in the window. A diner with red vinyl booths visible through foggy glass, a few pickup trucks angled into the lot. Normal and ordinary, a small town that existed in the margins of maps, noticed only by people passing through.

She wasn't passing through.

You're running, a voice in her head observed. It sounded like her mother. Calm, analytical, impossible to argue with. *You lost your job, lost your apartment deposit when you broke the lease, packed everything you owned into storage, and drove sixteen hours to a cabin you haven't seen since you were twelve. That's not grieving. That's fleeing.*

The voice wasn't wrong.

Meridian Aerospace had called it a restructuring. The HR representative had used phrases like "difficult economic conditions" and "no reflection on your performance" while sliding a severance package across the table. Two weeks after her mother's funeral. Two weeks after Zara had taken bereavement leave and returned to find her security badge deactivated and a cardboard box on her desk.

Six years at Pacific Tech. Four years at Meridian. All of it gone in the same month her mother stopped breathing in a hospital bed in Phoenix, her hand wrapped around

Zara's fingers as the monitors beeped slower and slower and then stopped.

The rental car drifted toward the shoulder, and Zara jerked the wheel back. She needed to focus. The turnoff should be coming up. Left onto a dirt road, then two miles to the cabin. Her mother's map was creased and soft from handling, the pencil lines fading but legible.

Great-Aunt Eleanor's cabin. Zara hadn't thought about the place in twenty years, not until the attorney had called to explain that Eleanor Henderson had died six months before Zara's mother and that the property had passed through the estate to its only living heir, Zara.

She found the turnoff and slowed, the rental car's suspension protesting as she left the pavement for packed dirt. Pines crowded close on both sides, their shadows long in the late-afternoon light. The air smelled different here, cleaner and colder. She rolled down the window an inch and felt goosebumps rise on her arms.

The cabin appeared through the trees like a memory surfacing. Single-story, dark-wood siding weathered to gray, a stone chimney rising from the center of the roof. The porch had a slight sag on the left side. The windows were dark.

Zara parked and sat with her hands still on the wheel.

The last time she'd been here, she was twelve. Her mother had driven them up for a week during summer vacation, and Zara remembered thinking the cabin was magic. Secret compartments and hidden rooms and stories her mother told about growing up, visiting Aunt Eleanor every August. They'd hiked the trails behind the property. Her mother had taught her to identify wildflowers. At night, they'd sat on the porch and counted stars.

That was before, the voice in her head said. *Before Dad left. Before Mom got sick. Before everything.*

She got out of the car.

The silence hit her first. No traffic noise. No neighbors. No planes overhead or construction in the distance. Just wind moving through pine branches and the distant cry of a bird she couldn't identify. Silence that filled your eardrums, that made you aware of your heartbeat.

Her engineer's brain began cataloging without permission. The roof appeared structurally sound, no visible sagging except for that porch corner. The chimney was intact, mortar lines showing age but no significant deterioration. One window on the south side had a crack running diagonally across it, probably thermal stress from Montana winters. The generator housing to the right of the cabin was rusted but present.

The front door was locked, but the key was exactly where the attorney had said it would be, under a ceramic frog missing half its face. Zara turned it in the lock and pushed the door open.

Cold air rolled out, carrying dust and the faint smell of mice and old wood and the particular scent of preserved time, the same one she remembered from her grandmother's attic. Preserved time and abandoned years.

She stepped inside.

Sheets covered the furniture, white shapes in the dimness that could have been ghosts or armchairs. The floorboards creaked under her feet. She saw mouse droppings in the corners, and when she tried the light switch, nothing happened.

The generator, of course.

Zara found it around the side of the cabin, a diesel unit about twenty years old, its housing spotted with rust but the mechanical components visible through the access panel. She pulled out her phone to use as a flashlight and crouched down to examine the problem.

The fuel line was cracked. The starter mechanism was seized, probably from sitting too long in cold weather without maintenance. The battery was dead. She could see exactly what was wrong, could visualize every step needed to fix it, and had none of the parts required to do so.

Great job, engineer, she thought. *You can diagnose the problem perfectly. You just can't solve it.*

She spent forty-five minutes trying anyway, improvising and attempting workarounds. By the time she gave up, her fingers were numb with cold and the sun had dropped below the tree line, leaving the cabin in shadow.

Inside, she found a cedar chest at the foot of what must have been the master bed, and inside that, blankets that smelled of mothballs but seemed clean enough. She wrapped herself in two of them and sat on the couch, the sheet pulled away to reveal faded floral upholstery.

She'd brought food. Not much, just road provisions. A can of tomato soup, her mother's favorite, which she ate cold, sitting in darkness, the spoon scraping against metal with each bite.

You should have stayed in Phoenix. You should have fought

for your job, or found another one, or done anything except run to a cabin in the middle of nowhere with no cell service and a broken generator and nothing but ghosts for company.

But she hadn't. She'd gotten in the car and driven away from it all, because staying meant facing the emptiness in her mother's apartment, the silence where her job used to be, and the terrible uncertainty of what came next.

She didn't know what came next.

For six years, she'd known exactly what her life looked like. Pacific Tech, then Meridian, then maybe Apex Propulsion or one of the startups that kept recruiting her with promises of stock options and flexible schedules. A career track with a clear trajectory. The life her mother had always wanted for her, stable, successful, and safe.

All of it had dissolved in a single month, and now she was sitting in a dead woman's cabin, eating cold soup in the dark, and she couldn't even muster the energy to cry about it.

The numbness had set in somewhere between the hospital and the funeral, and it hadn't lifted. She knew it was grief. She knew it would pass eventually, that she'd feel the full weight of her loss once the shock wore off. But for now, she felt empty. Hollowed out. Like a building with all the furniture removed, structurally sound but devoid of anything that made it worth entering.

She thought about her mother's hands. The way they'd moved when she was explaining a recipe, precise and confident. The way they'd felt in Zara's grip during those last hours, papery and thin, the bones too close to the surface.

I should have called more. I should have visited more. I should have been there when the diagnosis came instead of flying in after, always after, always too late for the things that mattered.

The guilt was familiar now. She'd been carrying it since the funeral, a constant companion that whispered accusations whenever she let her guard down. But tonight, in the dark, the cold, and the silence, she was too tired to fight it.

She pulled the blankets tighter and stared at the window, watching the last light fade from the sky.

That was when the headlights appeared.

Two beams swept across the cabin's front window, bright enough to make her squint after adjusting to the dark. An engine rumbled closer, the sound of tires on gravel, and then the world went quiet.

Zara was on her feet before she consciously decided to move. Her heartbeat accelerated from exhaustion to alarm in a breath. She didn't know anyone in Blackpine. She had no phone signal. No power. No weapon more threatening than a soup spoon.

Assess, her training kicked in. Security protocols from her work on classified aerospace projects. *Identify exits. Identify potential defensive positions. Do not panic.*

The back door. She'd seen it when she first entered, off the kitchen. If she moved quietly, she could reach it before whoever was outside reached the front porch.

But she didn't move.

Instead, she listened.

A car door opened and closed. Footsteps on gravel,

deliberate and unhurried. The creak of the porch steps, one, two, three, and then a pause.

A knock at the door. Three raps, spaced evenly.

Zara stayed frozen, blankets still wrapped around her shoulders, heart hammering against her ribs.

"Hello?" A voice, male, low. "Ms. Washington?"

He knew her name.

She took a breath and forced herself to approach the door. Through the gap between the curtain and the window frame, she could see a figure on the porch, tall with broad shoulders. The way he stood, patient and still, read as competent rather than threatening.

She didn't open the door.

"Who are you?"

"Reid Webb." The voice was calm, almost flat. "I'm with Blackpine Wilderness Rescue. Cole asked me to check on the new property owner. Make sure you got settled in okay."

She processed this. Small town. Word travels fast. Someone had probably seen her car at the gas station on the way in, or noticed an unfamiliar vehicle on the road. And if there was a local rescue team, they'd naturally be the ones to check on newcomers, especially those heading to isolated properties.

It made sense. It was logical. And she didn't open the door.

"The generator's broken," she said, because it was the first thing that came to mind. Practical and concrete, a problem with a solution.

A pause. "I can take a look at it."

She should have said no. She should have told him she'd handle it herself, that she didn't need help from a stranger who'd shown up unannounced at her door after dark. She was an aerospace engineer. She could fix a generator. She just needed parts.

But the cabin was cold, the night was closing in, and she was so tired that even the thought of turning him away required more effort than she could manage.

She opened the door.

OTHER FLORID ROMANCE BOOKS

To be notified of new releases and special promotions from Florid Romance, please join our email list:

https://floridromance.lmbpn.com/about/sign-up-for-our-news letter/

For a complete list of books published by Florid Romance please visit our website:

https://floridromance.lmbpn.com/

BOOKS BY RIVER TATUM

The Dating Diary

One is too Many BF's (Book 1)

Two Many Choices (Book 2)

Three is a Crowd (Book 3)

Four is a Disaster (Book 4)

The Dreamweaver's Pact

Whispering Dreams (Book 1)

Shattered Nightmares (Book 2)

Dawn Awakening (Book 3)

The Elemental Chronicles

Fire and Water (Book 1)

Earth and Sky (Book 2)

Chaos and Harmony (Book 3)

The Cursed Worm Court

The Healer and The Dragon (Book 1)

The Dragon's Bargain (Book 2)

Vows and Wings of Flame (Book 3)

Exile in Her Blood (Book 4)

Marked By Magic

Spellcasters (Book 1)

Tides of Fate (Book 2)

Final Spell (Book 3)

Crown of Lies

Princess with No Name (Book 1)

Prince of Shadows (Book 2)

The Crown Between Us (Book 3)

Wolves of Blackpine

Wild Heart (Book 1)

Restless Wolf (Book 2)

Shadow's Mate (Book 3)

BOOKS BY MICHAEL ANDERLE

CONNECT WITH MICHAEL ANDERLE

Website: lmbpn.com

Email List: michael.beehiiv.com/

Facebook: Facebook.com/LMBPNPublishing

Twitter/X: Twitter.com/MichaelAnderle

Instagram: Instagram.com/lmbpn_publishing/

Bookbub: Bookbub.com/authors/michael-anderle